The Pippington Tales

Book 1

The True Bride
And
The Shoemaker

By

L. Palmer

Emilee,
Thank you for your support on this
journey of ~~publishishing~~ publishing.
May your life be full of wonder
and magic.
J. Palmer

Copyright

Act I

The Shoemaker

Chapter 1

When Peter Talbot lifted the mound of dirt carrying a wild primrose, he was not thinking of magic and fairytales. His mind was filled with the fine curvature of Miss Adeline Winkleston's arches, of her small and delicate toes, of her dainty foot dangling from her fine ankle, of her smooth and perfectly proportioned heel. There were few pleasures greater than molding a shoe to cushion and support her feet.

The primrose's delicate petals swayed and danced in the wind as he patted the dirt into a pot and added water. Peter steadied his bowler hat over his thinning hair as he rose and looked out at the meadow. The field of daffodils was a pleasant sight, but hardly matched the lone primrose's fragile beauty. The flower would now have a better home on Adeline Winkleston's window sill, if the lady accepted it.

Peter meandered along the dirt path leading out of the meadow and onto the cobblestone streets of Pippington. The city had grown much in his twenty-five years. New automobiles puttered along while horses trudged on, pulling old, warped carts. The roar of a crowd echoed from the arena as men far braver than Peter raced dragons around the track. Even if Peter could afford a ticket, he preferred to avoid such spectacle. Though, today, racing a dragon seemed easier than approaching Adeline's door.

Peter kept on his path and walked past factories lining the edge of town, then by the old brick apartments and shops filling the southern region of the city. This was far from the northern bluffs, with mansions and high-rise penthouses rising over Chalice Lake. The cliffs dipped down and became the wharf

1

and docks filled with barges, fishing boats, and the common sort of people Peter understood.

Adeline herself was better than common. Her doorstep lay on Nightingale Lane, in the midst of Midtown, among the rows of tightly packed houses mixed in with banks, boarding schools, and professional firms. Each step of his polished shoes brought him closer to knocking on her door and speaking the words his sisters, Mary and Molly, had suggested: How are you Miss Winkleston? The weather sure is pleasant enough for a walk. Would you like to come? Any new hats catch your eye?

The last question had been suggested by Mary, whose husband owned Tevinson's Fine Hats. Peter was surprised Molly, whose husband owned Chancey's Dresses and Suits, didn't mention anything about clothing.

At last, Peter's feet pressed to the walkway outside Adeline Winkleston's house. He wiped sweat from his forehead and held the potted primrose in the crook of his arm. He had attempted to approach the doors of young women before, but had always retreated before reaching the porch.

To the flower, he said, "We'll have to do our best, I suppose."

Hoping he had not smudged anything on his finest dark coat and trousers, he approached the door. Molly had given his clothes a full examination before he left, including straightening his collar and polishing his buttons. A fine lady like Adeline would notice anything amiss.

Tensing the muscles of his face into something like a smile, he knocked on the door. He stepped back, holding his hat in his hand just as Mary had demonstrated. His cheeks ached as he kept his face in position as footsteps and giggling approached. He wished the hot summer day would turn cold so he could excuse his shaking legs.

Adeline Winkleston opened the door, her porcelain face aglow. A genuine smile began to warm Peter's cheeks, when the base tones of a man's voice echoed from the parlor. It was not her father's voice.

"Oh, good afternoon, Mr. Talbot," Adeline said. "Doing a bit of gardening, I see?"

"J-just passing through the neighborhood on my way home. Thought I'd make a house call to see if your new shoes are up to snuff."

Adeline's laugh rang out, sweet and light. She lifted her foot, the hem of her skirt slipping, revealing her ankle.

"I'm wearing them right now." She erupted into a batch of giggles that pelted Peter. "My fiancé, Nathaniel Bronhart, was just complementing the soft point of the toe. They are excellently made, as always, Mr. Talbot. We will surely be coming to you for…" She held a hand to her mouth as her eyes brightened. "The wedding."

"Congratulations." Peter's stomach attempted to join his feet on the ground. "Give my regards to Mr. Bronhart."

"Of course. Thank you, Mr. Talbot. Good afternoon."

The door shut, leaving Peter alone with his bowler hat and potted flower. He considered knocking and offering the plant as an engagement present. A burst of laughter from inside deflated the idea.

Peter's shoulders drooped as he kept hold of the potted flower and ambled along the lanes of Pippington. At last, he turned onto Dabbler Street and came to a friendly, aged building bearing a sign with a fine, sturdy gentleman's shoe above painted letters reading *Talbot's Boots and Other Footwear. We do repairs.*

Once inside with the door locked, having wasted a Sunday afternoon, Peter surveyed the empty shop. About a dozen pairs of his best boots sat on display in the window. Other shoes lay in various stages in the workroom downstairs. He walked past piles of leather and tools on his way to the cramped kitchen. He leaned his elbow on the counter and set down the flower. It was a delicate thing, too fine for the worn grooves of the wood it sat on. Perhaps one of his little nieces might like it and care for it.

He wandered upstairs, slumped on the edge of his child-sized bed, and stared at the door of his room since boyhood. When his father had died nearly a year ago, his sisters had told him to take the master bedroom and treat his room like the closet it was. However, the bedroom was where his mother and father had shared their lives. It was not his. His sisters' old room was now cluttered with pieces of junk. Going through the piles of broken chairs and rusted tools only brought ghosts of memories, days of working alongside his father. Someday, when he was ready, he'd take up his father's left over tasks. For now, he needed to keep the shop running.

As he slipped off his best suit and hung it up, he wished his mother hadn't died so long ago. He had been twelve and too young for her to explain women to him. His sisters reminded him daily of his promise to be married and have children to carry on the Talbot name. Yet, all he could talk to a lady about were her shoes and feet.

Evening ended its slow approach, and he ventured downstairs. Skimming through the newspaper, he ate the leftover soup and bread one of his sisters had left in the icebox. Judging by the burnt flavor, it was from Mary. He went ahead and ate as the clock ticked loudly on the windowsill. He left his dirty dishes in the sink. It was Molly's turn to look in on him tomorrow. She would give him a stern lecture about flies and mice coming because he didn't clean up after himself, and how he needed a wife to really take care of him. He'd stand there, his head scrunched toward his shoulders, waiting for the lecture to be over. Then, she would wash the dishes, do a quick sweep of the floors, and carry out Monday's washing.

Dinner complete, and the day ended, he returned to his room. Lying in bed, he hoped tomorrow would bring enough work to keep his mind off Adeline Winkleston's fine arches.

As the sun prepared to rise the next morning, Peter looked over the brief list of pending orders. It grew shorter every day. He needed to send his apprentice, Charlie, out to check on previous customers. There might be enough repairs or new orders to keep business steady a few more weeks.

Peter stepped into the kitchen and soon sat down with eggs, jam, and toast. His sister must have come early. The room was spotless, his dishes washed from the night before. She had even done so without waking him with her usual clattering and loud muttering. Returning to the shop floor, he noticed the primrose resting on the teller's counter. A band of sunlight pushed through the shades, illuminating the flower. It seemed to lean toward the sun, soaking in the morning light. His sister must have moved the flower so the pink-hue of its broad petals might add a touch of color to the room.

"Well, you do look nice today," Peter said to the flower as he dusted off the counter. "The shop's looking better than usual."

Soon his two workers, William and Caleb, entered. William gave a bright, "Hello," while Caleb only gave a nod and grunt. They both climbed down the ladder and into the basement workshop, just as they had every morning for fifteen years. Peter was often sure Caleb continued working more from habit than loyalty.

Peter was opening the shades when Charlie came sprinting in.

"Not my fault I'm late," the young man said. "Had to get the little brats in line for Mother. What's a fellow to do with all those brothers and sisters whining at him as he's trying to make a living? You understand, don't you?"

"It's all right," Peter said as he opened the last shade. "Just stay a bit late tonight."

Charlie slapped Peter's shoulder. "You're a swell fellow, you are, Mr. Talbot."

Peter restrained a sigh. His father would have bellowed at the boy, giving a speech about having respect for the trade.

Whenever Peter thought of getting mad, however, he saw the hollow cheeks of Charlie's younger siblings. They were healthier now that Charlie was employed, and Peter could not send Charlie off and let those children starve.

He unlocked the door and stood at the counter, waiting to greet any morning customers. Charlie busied himself with swatting flies as the morning wore on. Peter was sifting through the ledger when the bell rang, announcing a customer. He looked up as Mr. Rompell, Adeline Winkleston's foster father, entered.

Where his adopted daughter was light and airy, Rompell was a tall Sandarian, his skin still tanned from the deserts of his homeland. He always had the best appearance, his thick dark hair combed with polish, his suits tailored to his firm, lean build. He and his daughter made a handsome pair when they walked arm in arm. Peter smoothed his own thinning hair as he looked up at the man. How could Peter have thought to take the arm of such a man's daughter? This Nathaniel Bronhart was probably a better match.

Rompell set a pair of cracked boots on the counter. With a smile, he said, "Mr. Talbot, you have worked miracles with my shoes before, have you not?"

Peter turned the boots over. One's sole was split and the other's toe was wearing thin. "We can repair them, but it'll cost as much to make new ones."

Rompell tapped his gloved hands on the counter. "Your father gave me these when I first came to Pippington, when I had nothing." He smoothed his trimmed goatee before glancing at Peter. "I suppose, however, we must let go of things, now and then."

Peter set down the shoes as worn as the beggar Rompell had been years before. Rompell's coat had been patched and threadbare, his scarf moth-eaten, his pants stained and ill-fit. The man had worked hard to improve his station and now was a middle class landlord. If Rompell could rise so far, Peter could hold onto his shop.

"You've been a good customer a long time," Peter said. "I'll repair them, half-price."

Rompell flexed his fingers before turning over his hand, revealing a few coins. Peter smiled. He always enjoyed Rompell's little magic tricks and sleight-of-hand games.

"I can afford many things now." Rompell's eyebrow arched up. "Even a daughter's wedding. I'll pay full price for some new boots. It will help me keep up appearances of being a respectable gentleman."

Peter smiled, though he tried to forget his own faint hopes of Adeline's affection. "We'll get you set."

While Peter filled in the order sheet, Rompell leaned against the counter. He frowned as he picked up the primrose. With the blossom level to his face, he rotated it and sniffed it. "This is a peculiar flower, Mr. Talbot. Where did you acquire such a delicate thing?"

"The meadow heading toward Craggsville," Peter said.

Rompell set it down and ran his thumb along one of the petals. "What drew you to this one?"

"Well, I…" Peter rubbed his nose before admitting, "It looked lonely, out with all those daffodils. And… um… it brightens up the shop, doesn't it?" He gave a false smile.

Pulling his hand away, Rompell said, "It is a rare beauty. Do be careful with it."

"I'll be sure to."

Rompell set his hat on his head and looked to Peter. "Will the shoes take the usual amount of time?"

"Only a week or so."

"Business has been so slow?"

Peter shrugged. "It's a bright, warm day. Most folks don't worry about their shoes on days like this."

Peter smiled, hoping to believe the lie himself.

"I'll see if I can persuade my future son-in-law to pay a visit." Rompell began to step toward the door, but stopped to reach in his pocket. "I nearly forgot." He set down a canvas bag and opened it. Pulling out a small sphere wrapped in wax paper, he said, "You asked for some smoke snaps, to show your nephew."

Rompell tossed it toward the shop floor. Peter jumped as a plume of yellow smoke and sparks rose up before dissipating.

Peter grinned as he tucked the canvas bag under the counter. His sisters hated the snaps, but their anger was worth watching his nephew's eyes light up when the smoke and sparks rose up. "How much do I owe you?"

Rompell waved his hand. "Consider it a tip for your good service. I'll bring more next week when I pick up the shoes."

Rompell turned to the front door, when John Havish blustered in, carrying a load of new leather to deliver. The broad man stank of chemicals and animal fat as he slapped the pile down on Peter's counter. Peter grabbed the primrose before it could be knocked off.

"Good day, Mr. Talbot, Mr. Havish," Rompell said as he moved to step around Havish. However, the tanner reached out, grabbed Rompell's hand, and gave it a firm shake.

"Congratulations, Mr. Rompell!" Havish said. "I've heard Mr. Bronhart's a right good sort. I'm sure your daughter'll be quite happy."

"Congratulate me when the wedding is complete." Rompell grinned and slapped Havish's shoulder before heading out.

As the door shut, Havish said, "I remember when Miss Winkleston and my daughter Evelyn were school girls together. The girl was just a skinny little mite, and now look at her. She's a fine lady. This Bronhart better be as good a fellow as folks say."

Peter set the primrose on the shelf behind him and began checking the slabs of leather.

"How about you, Talbot? You find any nice girls to jaunt about with? It'll probably help you now that Bronhart's taken. Been too many doe-eyed glances in his direction. My Evelyn's seein' a good fellow herself, but I could have her invite a friend or two over for dinner, give you a chance to meet some nice girls and get out of the shop."

"Oh. I…" Peter looked out the window. "I've too much to do here."

Havish raised his eyebrow as he scratched his thick beard. "Seems quiet."

"Nothing unusual," Peter said.

Havish leaned on his pile of leather as he watched people pass the shop. "Look at them goin' by, with those factory-made shoes. I went and tried some, see what all the fuss was about. May as well drop a hammer on my toes. Felt shamed, really." He turned back to Peter. "How's it been on your business?"

Peter glanced at the ledgers, avoiding the knot trying to form in his stomach. "There's a few less boots going out, but we're getting a good number of repairs off the factory shoes."

He'd rather not admit there was barely enough in the till to pay for the week's wages and this set of leather. Beside the factories eating away at his business, many of his father's customers had died recently. Dead men did not come in for new boots.

Havish pulled on his beard as he eyed Peter. "You're a good fellow, Talbot, just like your pops. I'd hate to see your shop on hard times."

"We get by," Peter said.

With a grunt, Havish hefted a bright blue skin with strange markings from the middle of the pile. It gleamed, reflecting the dim light, a beauty in its strangeness.

"Got 'em from a man passin' through. Says it's griffin. Had Calman double-check it. This here's the real thing. Don't find beauts like this often."

"It's a fine piece. Would be wasted on the shoes I make," Peter said, checking the quality of the other skins. Maybe the blue leather would help build business, but Peter could not afford to try. Caleb had a wife to take care of now, William helped support his sister and her drunkard of a husband, and Charlie had his widowed mother and five siblings to help. Any funds had to go to them first.

9

"And good, sturdy shoes," Havish said. "I've had mine for ten years. Best boots in town, and at a good price, Talbot, but you'll never be able to compete with the price of boots comin' off the factory line. They're undercuttin' all the shoemakers in town.

"I told your pops for years that the real money's with those rich folks. A fine lady will buy six pairs of shoes in one go, and never wear 'em. I've been selling finds like this skin to Cordwainer up on the North End for years. His shoes are made for lookin', not for wearin'. He gave me one pair for my wife to thank me for a flap of dragon skin. She tried them on and said it was like gettin' her foot pinched between rocks. Went on to throw them at my boy when he got out of line, and the shoes are fallin' apart just from that.

"Now, if you got a shop up on the North End, and made boots half as pretty as Cordwainer's, I'd bet you could put that swine out of business. I only sell to him 'cause I can gouge the prices."

"If I were to make shoes like that," Peter said. "How would the rich ever see them?"

Havish raised a fat finger. "It only takes one customer, Talbot. One rich girl to see your shoes, and then go squealin' about 'em to all her friends."

"I don't know how to make fancy shoes," Peter said. "Just good, sturdy ones."

"You're a bright fellow. You'd figure it out."

"I really can't afford it, Havish."

Havish leaned back and mopped the constant layer of sweat off his forehead. He slapped the counter. "Talbot, you're a bleedin' heart, and I'm tryin' to help you out. Everyone around here knows you pay Charlie three times more than he's worth, and you sacrifice your own wages to pay Caleb and William, even if Caleb is an ungrateful wretch who—"

"He's my employee."

"Come on, Talbot. You keep him on 'cause you're a nice bloke. I've heard him down at McBriar's, blowin' on about how miserable he is here, and how he's a better business mind. And you keep this fellow on? I'd grab him by the belt and toss him down the street."

Havish tucked his thumbs in his pockets. "Tell you what, Talbot. You can't afford it right now, so pay me back once you've made a pair of shoes and sold 'em."

"No, please, Havish… I couldn't."

"It's only a loan, Talbot, and I'm insistin'."

Peter ran his hand over the leather as he found himself nodding. Havish punched his shoulder.

"You just wait and see, Talbot. I'm sure the shoes'll be a wonder."

Peter handed Havish the money for the leather, and the tanner left Peter staring at the blue skin. As if floating down from a cloud, a vision formed in Peter's mind of shoes fine enough for a lady, light and ready to dance away. His fingers curled around a pencil as he began drawing sketches and then scratching them out. He paused briefly for the two customers who dropped in for repairs. Once they were gone, he went back to churning through designs. His only reminder of lunch was Molly bustling in with two of her four children in tow.

Turning from his sketches, Peter hefted up the three-year-old Katie on his hip.

"How's the lovely girl?" he said.

She giggled as he swung her by the arms and set her down.

"What have I told you about swinging her around? She's not some rag-doll!" Molly shoved her six-month-old Benjamin into Peter's arms. "I'm running late because poor little Benji has been crying all morning, sick with something. But, I know how desperate you are when Mary or I miss checking in on you. Don't tell me how much of a mess you've made in the kitchen. I shall go face it myself."

"Mom, mom!" Katie said, pulling on her mother's skirt and pointing.

"Not now, Katie," Molly said, taking off her large hat and putting an apron on.

11

"The flower waved," Katie said.

Molly glanced at the flower. She looked to Peter. "Haven't got up the nerve to see Miss Adeline yet? Am I supposed to just drag you down there to get you to talk to the girl? Really, Peter!"

"I... I... I..."

"Out with it! Why can't you just speak like a man instead of stuttering all the time?"

He forced the words out in one breath. "She's engaged."

"I told you." Her finger waved dangerously in his face. "I told you to jump to it when you were first interested. Now, my Hubert came in and spoke his mind. He did no dilly-dallying. When you like a young lady, you've got to be a man and be aggressive. No wonder you missed out on Miss Adeline. I suppose I'll have to send over young ladies from the dress shop again."

Peter decided not to mention Molly had practically ordered Hubert to come to dinner for several months, before arranging for him to propose to her in what she presumed to be the perfect setting.

Molly stomped into the kitchen while Katie began chatting at the flower. Molly let out a scream and Peter nearly dropped his nephew. Charlie, Caleb, and William, who all had found work in the basement once Molly appeared down the street, came up to look.

Her hand laid across her forehead, her eyes wide, Molly approached Peter. He tried to back around the counter, but she pinned him in a corner and hugged him. Peter could not escape as she slapped his cheek with a wet kiss.

"Who's the girl?" Molly asked.

"Wha-what girl?" Peter said.

"The girl you cleaned the kitchen for? It's absolutely spotless! And that flower certainly brightens up the shop."

Charlie, Caleb, and William hid their sniggering as Peter stammered, "I-I thought you came this morning. It was like this when I woke up."

12

"Don't tease me." She began humming around the shop, seeking more signs of Peter's infatuation. She gasped as she picked up the blue leather. "This is very expensive! Are you preparing a present? What's her name? When is she coming by? I'm sure Mary'd want to meet her too."

"Th-there is no girl, Molly," Peter said, looking to his workers for help. They hid behind the staircase, hands over their mouths and cheeks red. None of them were brave enough to laugh in front of Molly, but all could barely hold their composure. "Mr. Havish gave it to me this morning, on loan."

"Mr. Havish always expects cash from my dear Hubert." Molly ran her finger along the luxurious leather. "How much did it cost you?"

"None of that now, Molly," Peter said. "I'm telling you the truth."

"You must come over for dinner tonight, Peter, and tell us all about her," Molly said. "I'll invite Mary and the children. Oh, dear, I must hurry then. I'll have to ask her to make something to bring. Can't do it all myself, you know, not with Katie and Benji to worry about. See you at suppertime, Peter. No later than seven."

Grabbing her hat, bag, and two children, she hurried out the door. As soon as she was a safe distance down the street, Charlie, Caleb, and William burst into laughter. Peter entered the kitchen and leaned his forehead against the wall. Taking a breath, he began to prepare himself for the long evening ahead.

Chapter 2

Once closing time came and his workers left, Peter took his time locking up the shop. Careful to keep the blue leather smooth and unblemished, he rolled it up and placed it in the spare room among the broken chairs. No one would bother looking in there. He went back downstairs, and looked for one more thing to do. However, every excuse to delay was gone. He pulled on his coat and hat and left the shop.

Though Molly lived a block south of Talbot's Boots, Peter travelled a few streets north to Durbin's Bakery. The bell cheerily rang as he entered, mixing with the hum of Mr. Durbin singing in the back of the shop. The bright-eyed Caroline Durbin looked up from wiping down the countertops.

"Good evening, Mr. Talbot. Which sister are you dining with tonight?"

Peter shuffled his feet. He stared at the young woman, noting again her rosy cheeks and pleasant brown ringlets hanging from her cap. Her figure was not perfect, but it was sturdy. He took off his hat and approached the counter.

"Both," he said.

"That'll be enough candy for all your nieces and nephews, then?" she said, already pulling out the paper bag. "Any special kind for tonight?"

"Just something that won't melt in my pocket, as usual, miss."

She took her time to weigh out a half-pound of sweets as she said, "Have you heard about Adeline Winkleston?"

Peter coughed as he looked down at his shoes. "I have."

"She came in this morning, showing off her ring while getting bread. It's a beautiful ring. Just beautiful."

"Of course."

"Would you like a loaf of bread to take with you to dinner? Half-price 'cause it's the end of the day."

"I suppose…" he said.

Caroline pulled out a round loaf and placed it in a larger paper sack. As she rung up the price at the register, she said, "My sister Nicole's been fawning over Mr. Bronhart ever since he was hired as an account manager at Mackabee and Sons. Says he has grand ideas of travelling the world as a professional dragon jockey. Just does it as an amateur now. Probably said those things to get attention from the local girls. Not as if he needs to. He's the sort of handsome you read about in stories. Dark looks, good mustache, nice, square jaw."

She told him the price, before going on, "I've told Suzie to stop mooning over him. He's just like our sister Georgina's husband. All talk and no bluster. Bronhart'll be lucky to get a promotion with how many sons and nephews Mr. Mackabee has. If he does go out and be some adventurer, he won't make a very good husband. Who will help with the children while he's off doing who knows what?

"Now, when I get married, it's going to be to a good, solid man. A fellow who makes a good living, and sticks to what's important. I don't need an adventurer. I need someone…" A warm smile softened the teasing glint in her eyes. "Someone like you, Mr. Talbot. Actually, I'm quite surprised there's not a line of girls at your door every day, trying to flirt with a good, respectable man like you."

"Oh… um…" he muttered, nearly dropping his cash as he handed it to her. "Thank you." He coughed. "Good evening, Miss Durbin."

He put the bag of candy in his jacket pocket, tucked the loaf of bread under his elbow and fumbled with his hat before putting it on. As he walked out of the store, Caroline leaned her elbow on the counter and rested her chin on her hand. Just before the door whooshed shut, Peter heard a long sigh.

Peter walked along the street, wondering if he had heard Caroline right. She had strange ideas of how women saw him, or if they saw him at all. He shook his head, and began picturing designs for the blue leather. Shoes were far easier to predict than women.

Upon arriving at Molly's, Peter gave his offering of bread. Dinner passed while Molly and Mary spoke over each other in a whirlwind of gossip, musing over who Peter should pine for next. Their husbands kept their heads down and focused on their plates. Peter watched the clock as he fidgeted with the mashed potatoes and slipped candy to his nieces and nephews. The minute hand took far too long as it ticked round the clock face, but, at last, it was late enough to politely leave. With the mystery of which girl was right for Peter still unsolved, Peter thanked his sisters for dinner and moved for the exit. His hand was nearly to the door, when Albert, Mary's husband, gripped his arm.

"Don't let your sisters choose who you marry," he whispered. "You don't want a wife like them."

He gave a sympathetic glance before slapping Peter's back and sending him out the door.

Once returned to the peace of his home, Peter took out the piece of blue leather. A shoe made of this could almost walk on air. He drew out another pattern, the lines seeming to drive themselves. Upon finishing, he looked over the pattern. The shoe would be soft, elegant, and would complement any lady's foot. However, these were not the sort of shoes made at Talbot's Boots. He crumpled up the paper and tossed it into the corner of the workshop. His imagination was getting the best of him. He rolled up the leather and put it away once more.

Tuesday morning, Peter stared at the grime-less window and gleaming floor. Neither had been so polished since his mother's death. It was among the things he and his father had neglected over the years. As Caleb came in, Peter said, "Did you clean the windows?"

Caleb glanced at the panes and laughed. "No."

Both William and Charlie answered no as well. Peter stared at the bright sun shining through the glass panes and reflecting off the floor. His sisters couldn't have done this. It wasn't like them. Maybe it was a kind stranger? But, if it was a stranger, how had they gotten into the shop?

He turned to the primrose. "Did you see anything?"

He grunted at himself as he unlocked the door. Perhaps a madness was settling in. Still, he would figure out who it was and thank them.

In the afternoon, Caroline Durbin stopped by with a pair of her father's boots. A hole had worn clean through the sole. Peter took the shoes and turned them over. Most boots brought in for repairs were layered with mud, but these had been freshly cleaned.

"Been a busy day at the bakery," she said. "Seems rather quiet here. Would you like me to put tacks on our shop floor so people's shoes wear out faster?"

"Tacks wouldn't hurt our shoes too badly," Peter said, tapping his fingers as he determined much work needed to be done.

"I was thinking," Caroline said as she leaned against the counter. "Wouldn't it be a wonder to make a shop where you can buy your dress, hat, and shoes, all to match, in one place? I think girls would spend all their money there." Her rosy cheeks rounded into a smile. "Have you ever thought of combining your shop with your two sisters' husbands' shops? It'd be…"

Peter dropped the boots as his whole body shuddered. It was terrible enough to have Mary and Molly checking on him every day, nagging him about his lack of a wife. If he let them have a say in his business, he would be trampled down, boxed up, and sat in the corner to quietly make shoes.

"Well, perhaps it's not such a grand idea, after all." Caroline gave a friendly laugh.

Peter attempted a polite smile before giving her the price for the repair. Her fingers brushed his palm as she dropped the money into his hand. Trying to ignore the tickling running up his arm, he said, "It'll take me a few days to do it. Thank you, Miss Durbin."

Her smile grew broader and she returned the thank you as she walked out the door. Peter rubbed his fingers together, Caroline's touch still lingering on his palm. The bell on the door rang and Peter shoved his hand in his pocket as Mary led her three children in. Both Hailey and Arthur tugged at Peter's jacket pocket, searching for candy.

"It's Caroline Durbin, isn't it?" Mary said, her eyes eager and bulging. She surveyed the floor. "Molly is right. You are cleaning up this place. Mother would be so proud of you. Miss Durbin is a sweet girl. I'll have her come round to dinner next Sunday, yes..."

Peter waved Hailey and Arthur away from his pockets. "I'm not in love with anyone."

"Oh, posh! Though, Sunday may be too late. She may find another man, like Miss Winkleston did. I think Friday will be better. Then you can ask her to a show..." She paused. "And that is a lovely flower. Molly was right. It does brighten up the room. Oh, I'm so proud of you, Peter!"

Mary put on her apron and cleaned as she sang in her nasal, warbling voice. Bowling past Peter, she greeted the two customers who came in.

Peter doubted Caroline would still suggest going into business with his sisters if she could see how people shied away from Mary.

At last, Mary left, the day wound down, and he sat alone to the dinner Mary had brought. He was glad for the quiet as he read the day's paper. After a while, he ventured upstairs and pulled out the blue leather. He ran his fingers over it, the vision of shoes walking on air returning. A woman danced in them, the shoes molded to her feet, her steps smooth and deft.

He went down to the workshop and whistled to himself as he pulled out his carpentry tools. He smoothed the edges of a block of wood, feeling the groove of the grain, forming it into the shape of a dainty female foot, the toes smooth, the heel rounded. As the night wore on, he sanded and smoothed until the clock rang a late hour.

He looked down at the last, the mold for the shoe. If someone wanted a pre-made shoe, they would go to the factory shops. The only advantage his shop had was making custom shoes. No one would buy these. He needed to spend his effort on more sensible things to build his business. He did not have time for such fancies.

However, the next morning, he went to the spare room to take one more look at the leather. It was worth the momentary dream. He had the leather. It couldn't hurt to make the shoes.

His heart jolted into his throat as he opened the spare room's door. The precarious towers of junk had been sorted and dusted, the floor swept, the cobwebs cleared. At the center of the room stood one of the old chairs, the legs repaired, the new finish still drying. He looked at his hands. There was no sign of paint or finish on them. He was not tired enough to have done this in his sleep. Yet, if someone else had done it, there should have been enough banging and thumping to wake Peter.

Perhaps one of his brothers-in-law had done it, but they were usually too exhausted by their wives.

In the evening, Peter stepped out to the brass shop and bought a large bell. He returned and hammered it on the door of the spare room. Even when he moved the door slowly, the bell clanged loud enough to bother the neighbors.

The bell gave him peace of mind as he took his weekly visit to the bar after closing. His drink remained full and forgotten as he lost himself in doodling out designs for the blue leather shoes. Other men called for him to play a card game, but he waved them off. He did not need to risk gambling away the little money he had. Instead, he returned home and set the leather on the work bench. With his chin resting on his hand, he stared at the blue skin. He spent the next hour was making the thick parchment staples to use as stencils for cutting out the leather. The actual cutting would wait. Dreams of shoes dancing did not bring in paying customers.

Thursday morning came, and Peter's new bell sat silent on the register counter. Peter ran back up to the spare room. The door was still locked and the box of leather was exactly as he had left it. His heart slowed to a regular rhythm as he rolled out the skin, just to be sure.

He was hardly aware of the last dropping from his hand and bouncing off his foot. Had he been too drunk the night before to remember doing this? However, he had hardly touched his drink. He shut his eyes. Sleep had to be lingering.

Yet, once he opened his eyes, the cut-out pieces of the shoes still lay in the bottom of the box. Each small detail and press was prepared for assembly. Determined to end this mystery, Peter spent the evening setting a rope across the top of the stairs. Once finished, he nodded to himself.

Friday morning, his foot caught in the trap, and he went tumbling down the stairs. He lay upside-down, his legs hanging in the air, hoping the damage wasn't too bad. As he rolled onto his feet and brushed off his clothes, he looked around the shop.

On the counter beside the primrose lay the blue shoes exactly as he had sketched them. The shoes were low-heeled, with ornamental holes along the edge. They were delicate in shape, seeming ready to go off dancing on their own. He analyzed and prodded them. These should have taken at least a few weeks to make, but were beautifully crafted and perfectly made in one night.

Peter hobbled up the stairs, his ankles and legs a bit sore. The spare room was still locked. He almost tripped on the rope again, but stopped to untie it. He went back downstairs and stood staring at the shoes as William came in, followed soon by Caleb.

"You all right there, Mr. Talbot?" William said. "I can open up while you get dressed."

Peter glanced down at his nightshirt. Being so improperly dressed might drive away the few customers he did have. He carried the shoes to his room and then changed. It took three attempts to properly button his shirt. He nearly gave up as his shaking hands fumbled with his shoe laces.

"Where's Mr. Talbot?" came Havish's booming voice.

Peter grabbed the shoes and ran down the stairs. William retreated to the workshop as Peter set the shoes on the pile of leather.

"These are even better than I expected, Talbot," Havish said. "You'd put Cordwainer out of business in a week! Let's put 'em in a window and see if they get sold."

"I... I didn't make them," Peter said, his voice hoarse. "Well, I made the last, and the stencils... but the sewing, the assembling... I didn't do it."

Havish picked up the shoes and turned them over. "Your workers did some fine work."

Peter shook his head, his skin feeling cold despite the warmth of the bright day. He stepped closer to Havish and whispered, "I woke up this morning and the shoes... they just appeared there, finished."

Havish frowned as he set the shoes down. With a laugh he said, "Maybe you did them in your sleep."

"I couldn't." Peter ran his hands through his hair. "There were at least a few more days of stages to finish the shoes, but it was all done in one night."

"One night?" Havish scratched his beard and grunted. "Maybe it sewed itself? It is griffin hide."

Peter pulled the shoes from Havish's thick hands and rested them on the counter beside the primrose. "I don't think so."

"Well, if no one's willin' to claim credit for such good work, go on and sell 'em," Havish said. "Put it in your window. I'll spread the word you've got 'em."

Not knowing anything else to do with them, Peter put them on a box in the window.

The day wore on with women lingering as they strolled past, giving the shoes a longing glance before carrying on. By afternoon, small crowds formed around the bright blue shoes next to all the black and brown work boots on display. None of the people came in the store.

Peter closed the shutters at the end of the day, blocking the view of the remaining bystanders. The evening passed far into night as he leaned on his elbow and stared at the shoes. Someone had to have made them. Perhaps they would make another. He set out a pair of unfinished shoes and said to the primrose, "You'll keep an eye on that, won't you?"

Saturday morning came and the unfinished shoes lay just as he had left them. The puzzle ran through his mind as he did odd jobs around the shop to pass the day. Most of them had already been done by whoever had been sneaking around and helping him. He forgot about his dinner plans until Molly appeared in the afternoon.

Handing him his freshly pressed and starched shirt, she said, "Those shoes are beautiful, Peter. See what a woman's touch can do in your life? Good topic for dinner with Miss Durbin tonight."

He took his time dressing. Caroline Durbin was a nice girl. He had to be sure to look fine and not let his mind wander off and ponder the blue shoes. As he went to leave, he paused beside the delicate primrose on the counter. He had potted it for Adeline, but perhaps it was meant for Caroline. He began to reach for it, but stopped. He'd grown accustomed to it sitting on the counter. It was a small spot of beauty in his old shop, and he would be sorry to part with it.

Instead, he tipped his hat to the primrose and said, "Wish me luck."

It was a longer walk than usual to Durbin's Bakery. Caroline beamed from behind the counter, her hair carefully curled and pinned.

"I knew you'd stop by here first." She held out a bag with candy in it. "It's my gift for tonight."

He tried to pay, but she laughed and shook her finger at him. As she came around the counter, he slipped some coins beside the register. She took off her apron and pulled a coat over her plain, nice dress. Her only ornament was a broach at her neck.

"Papa! We're leaving," she said.

"Have a good time," her father said from the back.

Peter turned toward the door. Caroline bent her arm, clearly waiting. He stared at her elbow, his arms frozen to his side. Somehow, he worked up the strength to offer his arm. With a broad smile, she hooked her elbow through his, and they walked to Mary's apartment.

Mary held back her own conversation, allowing Caroline time to speak. It was a rare occurrence. Caroline laughed politely and tried to engage Peter in conversation. He gave only one- or two-word answers. The dinner wore on, and he found himself answering with a whole phrase, and then a whole sentence without stuttering. Caroline was not as beautiful as Adeline, but she treated his nieces and nephews well, and talked politely to his sister. Those were admirable qualities.

The platters of food were nearly empty when Mary pulled out a pair tickets.

"Oh, Albert, I'm afraid I forgot to ask Molly to come and watch the children. We won't be able to go, but I hate to waste these tickets to Alvin Westengaard's lecture tonight." She smiled at her brother and batted her eyes. "Peter, would you mind taking Miss Durbin?"

Albert grunted and rolled his eyes. Caroline's eyes brightened and Peter tried to hold a polite smile as he accepted the tickets.

They walked together a few blocks and then rode the trolley, Caroline chatting on about how nice his sister seemed. He decided to let her learn the truth later. Once in their seats, Peter tried to stay awake as the handsome author's baritone voice read out passages in his book. Peter's fingers gripped the chair as Caroline leaned on his arm. She listened intently, tears in her eyes as something tragic and romantic happened. Peter couldn't tell what because he had nodded off. He clapped alongside the crowd as Westengaard came to a triumphant finish, and Caroline cried, "Bravo!"

On the journey back, Caroline said, "He was magnificent wasn't he? But I wouldn't want such a troubled romance. I like everything good and steady."

Once on her parent's doorstep, Caroline beamed at Peter and said, "Papa said I could invite you to dinner for tomorrow night. Would you like to come, Mr. Talbot?"

Peter stood still, hoping his ears were working. Women never invited him to anything other than to repair their shoes. However, the words were real and true. He found himself smiling and giving her a nod. "That sounds nice, Miss Durbin."

"I'll see you then." She squeezed his hand before disappearing into the house.

He stood on her doorstep a few moments, trying to remember how to move his feet. He took a breath and strolled back to his shop, all thoughts of Miss Adeline Winkleston being washed away by the image of Miss Caroline Durbin.

Chapter 3

Peter stood before the Durbin residence on Sunday evening and stared at the door. So far, he did not hear any giggling or young men's voices. He pulled at his collar and took a few breaths before stepping on the doorstep. He raised his hand to knock, when the door flew open.

"Well hello, Mr. Talbot," Mrs. Durbin said. She gripped his shoulders and kissed his cheeks. "It's a mighty pleasure to see you."

Mr. Durbin crowded into the doorway to gave Peter a firm handshake and a grin.

Peter handed the smiling Caroline the flowers he had bought as he said, "I... it's... I'm glad to... Good evening."

She blushed. "Thank you, Mr. Talbot."

They walked together to the dining table and the meal began.

It had been a long time since Peter had gone to dinner without his sisters talking over their husbands. He laughed at Mr. Durbin's jokes, most of which were puns about bread and dough, and found his own answers extending into complete sentences. Caroline and Mrs. Durbin's chatting filled most of the evening. However, their conversation was sweet, their topics kind, and the night all-around pleasant. After dinner, a game of cards was played and the meal was capped off with a succulent apple pie.

Caroline laughed nervously as her father said, "This girl's a fine cook. If she opened her own shop, she could put me out of business."

At the end of the evening, Peter stood on the doorstep and found himself saying, "Perhaps we should do this again?"

"Next Sunday?" she said. "With my parents again? They would be happy to have you over."

"Yes... yes, of course."

His feet were light as he whistled his way home. He returned to the shop, and went to bed in a daze. He smiled up at the ceiling as he drifted off to sleep, the blue leather shoes forgotten for one night.

Rapid pounding echoed through the shop, waking Peter and sending him tumbling from his bed. He staggered down the stairs and walked to the front door. He raised the shutter and discovered a woman standing outside, her clothing finer than anything he had ever seen. He fumbled with the lock as he said, "We're not open yet."

The woman raised her narrow chin. "I am Mrs. Leticia Hampnell of Talcourt. I came to inquire about those fine shoes in the window."

She tapped on the pane with the ivory handle of her cane.

"Pardon me, ma'am," he said, trying to be composed while standing in his nightshirt. "We haven't opened yet. If... if you'll give me a moment... just a moment to... um... dress, I will be with you."

He opened the door and let her in. "Just a moment."

He sprinted up the stairs, and grabbed the nearest clothing. Tucking in his shirt, hoping it was on straight, he came tumbling back down the stairs.

Mrs. Hampnell adjusted the small hat decorating her gray-streaked hair as she waited.

Smoothing down his own hair, Peter said, "The name's Peter Talbot, ma'am. I'm the owner of the shop, ma'am... I..." He stopped as he retrieved the shoes. It would be better to be silent and let the shoes speak.

The gentlewoman sat in one of the waiting chairs, her bustle occupying most of the seat. She held her foot out. Peter knelt and unlaced the high-heeled, overly-pointed boot.

"Is this boot a bit wobbly and tight?" he said.

"Why yes," she said. "If they weren't so beautiful, I would never wear them. But, all in the name of fashion."

He ran his hands over the stiff sole and rigid leather. "These don't breathe very well, do they?"

"I am here regarding those blue shoes, sir."

He hesitated before saying, "If you want to drop the boots off for a day or two, I can keep them looking good, but make them feel much more comfortable."

She glared at Peter. "No one tampers with a Cordwainer shoe."

"Sorry. Of course... of course ma'am." He held out the blue shoe. "These aren't designed for your feet, so they'll not fit right, but it looks like you're close to the same size. Each pair of shoes coming out of Talbot's is one of a kind, ma'am, one of a kind."

"Mr. Cordwainer says a foot will mold itself to the shape and beauty of the shoe. Fit is relative."

Peter tried to keep the bewilderment from his face as he muttered, "Oh." He considered his words carefully before saying, "But, no mean to offend you, ma'am, nor criticize Mr. Cordwainer's fine work. I just... believe shoes should be molded to the foot of the owner. Feet themselves shouldn't be forced into unnatural shapes. It's all about the last—"

"The what?"

"The last. It's a mold for the shoe. Have you ever had one made for you?"

"Mr. Talbot, the blue shoes, please."

Peter clamped his mouth shut as he attempted to place the shoe on her foot. It took some tugging, and scrunching of her toes, but he got it on. She admired it with a smile, saying, "Well, that is beautiful, but no better a fit than Cordwainer's."

"That's because I made it for another woman's feet," he said.

"Whose, I pray? I think I shall steal her feet. They are so dainty."

Peter kept his eyes on the shoes as he said, "No one, really. It was just an experiment." He carefully removed the shoe, making sure to not tug on her toes and heel. "If you really like them, ma'am, I've got enough leather to make a pair just for you." Remembering what Havish told him, Peter said, "It'll be a bit different than these, but still nice, and they'll fit your feet like a tailored glove."

"And what is your price?"

Peter quickly calculated the price of the leather. She could probably pay that much. Plus, he did need to cover man hours. Such shoes would need at least a week, with going through stages. When he was finished, he tried not cringe as he named a price far higher than he had done before. They would probably talk down from there.

Mrs. Hampnell's face scrunched in consideration as she held the blue shoe in her hand. Peter's heart began to droop as he realized she was going to reject such a high price. Then, she said, "Cordwainer would charge at least three times that much for the same shoes. I think I'll give you a try, Mr. Talbot. Is half up-front satisfactory?"

"Of course," he said all too quickly, his voice high pitched.

Caleb arrived as Peter pulled out his measuring tools. He scowled from the door, as if Mrs. Hampnell was a foreign beast. Peter handed Caleb the notebook and had him write the measurements down as they were pronounced. Peter ran his hands along her foot, feeling the contours of the arch, the toes, the heel. The arch was bent high, and the toes permanently cramped from Cordwainer's shoes.

When he was finished, Mrs. Hampnell signed her contract, and made the promised payment from a beaded handbag. Peter and Caleb stared at the stack of money as she left the shop.

That was as much as they usually made in a week. Unable to stop himself, Peter let out a whoop of joy.

"Where'd all that come from?" Charlie said as he came in.

Peter left Caleb to explain as he shoved the money in his pocket. He ran down a series of streets till he reached Havish's tanning shop. He burst in the front office and asked for Havish. The tanner came in, and Peter threw the bag to Havish as he said with a grin, "There's my down payment on the blue leather. The rest will be coming in a week."

"You sold those shoes?"

"No. I'll not be Cordwainer and make excuses to sell shoes that don't fit. But, I was able to sell Mrs. Hampnell shoes custom made for her."

Havish laughed as he dropped the bag on his money counter. He and Peter counted the money again. Putting it into the till, Havish punched Peter's shoulder. "Excellently done, Talbot! Tell me when you need more fancy leather, and I'll get it to you."

The rest of the day, Peter molded the last, carving it to perfectly support Mrs. Hampnell's high arches and wide heel, giving enough space to let her toes spread out properly. He drew out the plans, whistling happily. Tomorrow, they would be able to cut out the design, and the sewing could begin.

He went to bed, hoping Havish was right. In the morning, he whistled to himself as he walked to the counter to look over the plans for Mrs. Hampnell's shoes. He wanted to be sure he was satisfied with them.

There, sitting on Caleb's workbench, sat the fully completed shoes.

He picked them up. The craftsmanship was expertly done. The stitching matched the style of the other pair of shoes. He turned them over, analyzing the sole. They would match the shape of Mrs. Hampnell's feet perfectly.

Peter carried them up to the main floor and set them on the counter. As Charlie, Caleb, and William came in, they joined Peter in staring.

"If it's none of us," William said. "Who's coming in?"

Charlie laughed. "Maybe there's a ghost."

Though it had been said as a joke, Peter wondered if it was a ghost. His mother never helped make shoes. His father believed fancy shoes were a waste of leather, and only made shoes for work. If his father was a ghost, he would balk at these shoes. Peter did not want a spirit he was unfamiliar with to be running around his shop.

They decided not to deliver the shoes yet. He did not want to give Mrs. Hampnell too high of expectations. He would wait till Thursday.

Tuesday and Wednesday passed with the shop running as usual, and no new repairs or magically appearing shoes. Havish, however, stopped by with a theory.

"Been readin'," he said, waving a book titled Explaining the Unexplainable. He opened it to a chapter called "How to Manage Magical House Guests" and jabbed his finger at a picture of little elves hammering a shoe. "You've got an elf problem."

Peter stared at the illustration. "I don't think…"

Havish pointed to a paragraph.

> *Now and then elves like to help the downtrodden to increase their business. However, if the elves are not appreciated properly, they will one day disappear. In order to prevent this, leave them small gifts and treats every night. Their particular favorite is pastries.*

"Elves and magic don't exist," Peter said.

"How do you know?" Havish said. "You can't explain how those shoes came about. Who do you think made them so fast? It's got to be magic, and elves seem to like shoes."

Peter scratched his head.

"How about this?" Havish said. "We'll do a test. You set out a plate of pastries. If the pastries are still here in the morning, we'll look for other answers. If the pastries are all gone and eaten, then it's got to be elves."

Peter nodded numbly as he looked at the picture. He would prefer having elves in his house over ghosts.

As Caleb and William closed the shop, Peter went to Durbin's Bakery. Caroline beamed as he walked in, distractedly finishing with her current customer. Peter nodded at her and fiddled with his hat as he waited his turn. Caroline remained polite while rushing the next few customers.

As Peter stepped to the counter, she said, "You're here early. Are you having dinner with your sisters tonight?"

She was already reaching for the candy bags, when Peter said, "No. I... er... My employees have been working hard, so I thought I'd... er buy some pastries for them."

Caroline pulled out a pastry bag as she asked, "How many? Three?"

Peter drummed his fingers on the counter as he said, "Make it... five. An extra one or two. Charlie's a growing lad, you know."

He paid for the pastries while attempting to return Caroline's glowing smile. With an awkward tip of his hat, he left and returned to his closed shop. He searched for his least chipped plate and wiped it off before setting out the pastries. Carrying it into the shop, he presented it to the primrose.

"What do you think?" He dropped it on the counter. "I must be a fool."

The door swung open as Molly arrived to drop off his dinner.

"Saw you leaving Durbin's Bakery," Molly said. "Had to check on what's in the shop?"

Peter stared down at the pastries as she pattered him with questions, never taking a breath for him to give an answer. Once she left, he slumped into the chair behind the counter.

"What would you do with sisters like that?" he said to the flower. He poured a little water into the soil. "I'm sure your sisters are as lovely as you are."

As the sun rose Thursday morning, the pastries were gone. The plate was washed and placed back in the cupboard. He looked to the primrose, but the flower had no answer. Perhaps it was elves.

Giving himself some time to think, he walked slowly to Durbin's Bakery and bought the same amount of pastries. If it were elves, he did not want to upset them. Who knew what an angry elf would do?

Caroline eagerly assisted him and said, "Why don't you stop by for lunch today? My father wouldn't mind."

"I wouldn't!" Mr. Durbin yelled from the kitchen.

"Oh. I... er... I've a delivery to make," Peter said.

"How about tomorrow?" Miss Durbin said.

He tried to smile. "That'd be nice."

He began to walk out, when Caroline called after him and held up the forgotten bag of pastries.

In the afternoon, Peter left William in charge as he rode the trolley north across the city to Mrs. Hampnell's mansion. He held the plain wooden box under his arm as he passed gilded window panes, beveled columns, and marble entryways, all gargantuan. He eyed the statues looking down at him from granite pillars, their blank eyes following him. Pulling at his collar, he wondered if he should have worn a better suit.

Once at Mrs. Hampnell's mansion, the housekeeper led Peter along a long, polished hallway and to a sitting room. His whole apartment above the shop could fit in it. Mrs. Hampnell sat on a fine couch, a small herd of terriers resting around her feet. Rich green velvet was draped along the walls and an ornate Sandarian carpet drowned the floor in color. Peter gripped his hat and box before forcing himself to enter.

"Work went quicker than expected," he said as opened the box and presented the shoes.

Mrs. Hampnell gasped as she lifted the delicate blue shoes from the box. "So simple, yet so beautiful. I have never seen a shoe like them."

Peter slipped them easily on her feet. Her eyes widened as she lifted her leg and flexed her foot.

"It is a wonder," she breathed.

"You can't know a shoe till you've walked in it," Peter said.

Mrs. Hampnell rose and took a few tentative steps. She paused and stood still, as if discovering a new sensation. Peter pulled on his ear and gave one more glance at the shoes. They looked up to his standard. He hoped there wasn't anything wrong.

"Oh!" she cried as she took a few long strides. "Oh, how wonderful!"

She let out a girlish spurt of laughter, unbefitting her dark dress and gray hair, and spun across the floor, scattering the dogs. Arriving in front of the full length mirror, she lifted her skirts and pointed her toe.

"These are marvelous! I've never worn shoes so comfortable, yet so beautiful!"

Peter started as Mrs. Hampnell leaped over to him and clasped his hands. "Your price is far too low, Mr. Talbot. I must double it."

"But... that's not the contract. I couldn't."

"Oh, posh!" She waved her hand. "I've already wasted too much on Cordwainer's bricks. Fifteen years I've been going there, not knowing what marvelous shoes existed! My eyes are open now, Mr. Talbot. It is my duty to liberate the feet of the women of this city."

"I really don't think..."

"Consider it a tip, then," she said, once again admiring her feet in the mirror.

The envelope of money weighed Peter down as he took the long walk back to the trolley and then his shop. William was closing the shutters as Peter entered.

"Wait a moment," Peter said.

William joined him at the counter as he spread out the cash. William's eyes bulged, his face turning red as if he could not breathe.

"What'll we do with all that?" William said.

"We'll save it for now, I suppose," Peter said. "And hope things keep up."

"And what if they do keep up?"

Peter rubbed his forehead. "I don't know."

With William gone and the money in the safe, Peter set out the pastries for the night. As he watered the primrose, he said, "Tell the little fellows thank you for me."

Friday morning, Peter went once again to buy pastries. Caroline had the order ready as she said, "I hoped you'd come in. Business doing well?"

"Seems so." He returned her grin and then went back to the shop.

A half-hour before opening, two women in fine clothes knocked at the door. One was graying and plump, the other was blonde and well-curved. Glad his workers were already there, Peter opened the door and welcomed them in.

"We were at dinner last night with Mrs. Hampnell," the elder woman said. "And she showed us her marvelous shoes. Weren't they marvelous, Amelia?"

"Oh, yes Mother. Just marvelous."

"Amelia, here, is just beginning to attend balls, and can hardly endure dancing the whole evening."

"It is far too much. My feet ache so terribly that I must sleep all the next day."

"When Mrs. Hampnell spoke of how comfortable your shoes are, we just had to come and see this wonderment for ourselves."

Amelia walked to the window and squealed with delight. "These shoes are so beautiful. I must have a pair just like them."

Peter measured their feet and took their orders while Charlie snuck an extra glance at the young woman's ankle. As the women were sent on their way, the elder woman handed Peter her card.

"If these are everything Mrs. Hampnell says, I shall put a good word in my column for *The Rosetown Journal*," she said.

Peter stared at the filigreed card. His sisters read *The Rosetown Journal* every week, taking in all the gossip as if they were part of the inner circles of the upper class.

As she gathered her fur coat around her shoulders, she said, "The word of Petunia Ophombach is like gold among high society, my young man. I trust the shoes will be remarkable."

With the pair of ladies gone, Peter set about making the lasts. Then, another deluge of aristocratic customers came in. By noon, Peter had a stack of fifteen orders. He had Caleb helping him measure feet while William continued working down below.

In the afternoon, Peter sent Charlie to Havish with an order for more leather. On the bottom of the sheet, Peter wrote: *You were right. Thank you. There'll be more to come, I hope.*

The afternoon stacked up twenty more orders. Hopefully, the customers would return, and the time it took to make the last would be worth it. Each order got told a further and further date for delivery. With or without the elves' help, it would take a while to make so many fine shoes.

Peter deposited the gold at Abbott's and Sons, keeping enough to pay Havish for the leather coming in the morning. Pondering how to keep up with so many orders, he turned onto the street where Durbin's Bakery lay.

His lunch date with Caroline. He had forgotten.

He sprinted down the street until reaching Durbin's Bakery. It was closed.

Gulping in air, he ran to the Durbin's house and pounded on the door. He stood back, panting, until Mr. Durbin opened the door and glared.

"Look who's turned up," Mr. Durbin said.

"I'm sorry," Peter said, still out of breath. "I-I was so busy... I forgot."

"You forgot?" Mr. Durbin folded his arms. "My daughter could barely work because of her tears, Mr. Talbot. If you want to toy with my daughter's heart just to get some free pie, you can go to another bakery."

Peter tried to catch his breath, tried to think of an answer, tried to form words.

"And you can find another girl to take to the dance Saturday and break her heart, and don't even think of joining us for Sunday dinner."

"What? The dance Saturday? Wait... It... it was just a mistake, Mr. Durbin... I lost track of time..."

"Well, I don't want my daughter going to dances with men who can't manage a pocket watch!"

"Please, Mr. Durbin..."

"Goodnight, Mr. Talbot." The door slammed and the lock clicked shut.

Peter let out a sigh as he tucked his hands in his pockets and turned away. He paused and glanced up at the second story window. There seemed to be a face looking out, but it was gone when he glanced again.

Once back at his shop, the loneliness of the work room began closing in around him. He busied himself with carving lasts and drawing designs. There was more work than even the supposed elves could help with. After a while, he brought down the primrose and set it on the bench. The flower was slim and delicate, but made the workshop seem a bit warmer.

Falling into the rhythm of carving lasts, he began to tell the primrose of his day and Caroline.

"What am I supposed to do? I just missed a lunch with her. I've got a business to run. She is a nice girl, though. I would like a bit more time with her."

Before heading to bed, he placed the primrose back on the counter, and set out half of the pastries he had bought in the morning. He stored the other half, unsure if he would ever be able to buy from the bakery again. On Saturday morning, six pairs of completed shoes sat on the counter. Slips of paper were set in the shoes, with the names of customers written in childish, poor writing. It was barely legible. Beside them, lying on the cleaned pastry plate, was a note that said: *By hur flours*.

Peter frowned, taking a moment to decipher the words. It appeared good advice. Sitting to breakfast, he contemplated his options. His thoughts were cut off as the shop's door banged open and Mary came bursting in.

"After all Molly and I have done for you," she said, her face red as she stood over him. "You go and break poor Miss Durbin's heart. Mother didn't raise you to be a cad. Simply because you have wealthy customers at your door doesn't mean you should run about, breaking the hearts of poor, common girls like Miss Durbin!"

"I-I…"

"I've told you to stop stammering like a fool, Peter."

"I- I tried to apologize last night… Her father wouldn't let me."

"Good! He'll show you how to treat a lady." She reached in her bag and pulled out a pair of tickets. "Now, you march over there and use these to apologize."

Peter took the tickets. They were to a dragon racing match that afternoon. Holding them out to Molly, he said, "I don't even like dragon racing."

"It is not about what you like. It is about charming and impressing the lady."

"Right, then," Peter muttered.

He hurried to the florist's first. As the woman who ran the shop gathered a bouquet of gerberas, she said, "Miss Durbin always admires these."

Wondering how far the gossip had spread, Peter hid the flowers under his coat and walked to Durbin's Bakery. He stood at the door and took a deep breath. The eyes of the customers were on him as he stepped inside, holding the bouquet of flowers like a shield. Caroline raised her chin and focused on the next customer. She took her time with each one, purposefully never looking at Peter as the line shortened.

As he reached the counter, she slapped a bag of day old pastries down in front of him.

"If this is all you came for, you may take them."

"I... er..." Peter swallowed before pushing the flowers forward. "These are for you."

"They are beautiful," she said. Her cheeks warmed into a teasing smile. "I will accept them if they come with an explanation."

"I am... sorry, miss, for the... er... misunderstanding yesterday... I... you see... er... I lost track of time. The shop's been busier than usual. I'd be honored if you'd... um... go with me to the..." He pulled out the tickets Molly had given him and read, "The dragon races."

"There's also a fine dance at McBriar's tonight," her father called from the kitchen.

"And, yes, a dance... if that's what you'd like..."

Caroline took the flowers as her smile warmed. "If you do need to cancel again, do try to send a message." She drank in the scent of the flowers before saying, "I gladly accept."

Peter's feet felt light as he returned to the shop. He paused at the counter and wrote a note to the elves:

Thank you. The flowers worked. More pastries to come.

He went to get dressed, when he realized his best suit had a hole in the elbow. As he sat down to try to sew it, he thought of all the money he had sitting at Abbot's and Sons. Though his palms sweated the whole time, he went to the bank, and then to Chancey's Dresses and Suits. He was glad his sister wasn't there as Albert quickly fit him into a fine suit.

Peter's heart pounded as he paid an extra fee for the quick work. For so long, he had held onto his money, carefully counting each penny. Yet, today, he had enough.

Taking the money, Albert grinned. "Hopefully, your good fortune will spread to the rest of us."

Peter tried to smile back.

Soon, Peter returned to the bakery. Caroline set aside her work apron, and put on a straw hat with feathers on it. She did look nice.

She gave his suit an admiring glance and they walked to the arena together. The dragon races were as heart-pounding as usual, with the giant beasts flying wing to wing, snarling and growling while their riders gripped tightly to their saddles. Peter found his stomach flipping along with the dragons as they did turns and loops, all to drive past their opponents. Caroline laughed and cheered, joining the excitement of the crowd. Peter found it easier just to watch her.

They had a quiet dinner afterward, and then went off to dance at McBriar's. Peter's feet tripped more than they danced, but Caroline only laughed sweetly and continued as if nothing had happened. He laughed with her, his pulse quickening as his palm pressed to hers.

When they returned to her doorstep, she lingered and chatted. Peter held his bowler hat in his hand as he wondered what a fellow was supposed to do at this point.

As the clock inside rang a late hour, he said, "Well, I'd best be going."

"You are joining us for dinner tomorrow, aren't you?" She squeezed his arm.

Peter found himself smiling. "If you'd like... yes."

Caroline returned his smile as she entered the house. Peter whistled once more as he walked home. His shop was at last doing well, there was a girl who he had a good chance for a future with, and life was overall pleasant. As he stepped into his shop and locked the door, he looked to the primrose.

"Thank the elves for me, won't you? I'm sure they're a swell batch of fellows.

Act II

The Guest

Chapter 4

Summer faded into autumn, and then winter draped the city in snow and frost. One evening, Peter stood alone in his shop, thumbs tucked in his suspenders, as he admired the windows. There, in bold, freshly painted letters, was the name of his store. It was a project he and his father had discussed for a long time, but there were never enough funds. Now, six months since the day Havish had brought the blue leather and the elves had come, he had enough funds to buy a whole other shop.

Success, however, did not ease the loneliness pressing in around him at night. Even knowing the elves were at work downstairs, he lay in bed feeling the emptiness of his apartment. He knew the remedy his sisters would suggest, if they knew the problem. Over the past few months he had thought it through while attending dinner at the Durbin's and escorting Caroline to recitals, festivals, and dances. Others might seek a romantic adventure, but he'd rather stay with a nice, respectable girl like her.

Locked in the shop safe was the ring he had bought from Lapidary's. Tomorrow night, he would host a High Winter feast at the Gormond with his sisters, workers, Havish, their families, and Caroline herself. He had left an invitation for the elves, but doubted they would show themselves. No good being ungrateful, though.

Again, he tried to envision the end of the evening. In front of friends and family, he would kneel before Caroline, and invite her to take a permanent position in his life. However, all was a gray haze as his palms sweated and his knees shook.

He paced the floor again, running his thumbs along his suspenders. Stopping in front of the primrose, he said, "How about this? 'Caroline, I like you a lot. You're a nice girl. Will you... will you...'"

His mouth was dry and his throat clenched around the words. The town bell rang a late hour, and he trudged up the stairs. Sleep might bolster his courage. However, the clock in his room ticked on loudly and he tossed about. He threw off the blankets and stared at the ceiling, deciding a late-night snack might help bring rest.

He walked down to the kitchen and opened the door. A dim whirring and tapping ebbed in the room. He squinted in the darkness. Light shone through the cracks of the trapdoor leading to the workroom.

It was the elves. It had to be. If he intruded, they might disappear. Yet, after six months, one look couldn't do too much harm. He might meet them, and thank them, and find out what pastries they liked best. He lit the lantern beside the counter and held it as he opened the trapdoor and crept down the stairs. He stopped as one of the steps creaked.

The light in the workroom went out. Peter leaped down the last few steps. Hopefully, he had not insulted them. He passed three finished pairs of shoes on the worktable, next to a half-finished pair and abandoned tools. As he stepped further in, his lantern illuminated the corner.

Crouched in the corner like an injured animal was a young woman of no more than twenty. Her figure was long and willowy, her skin pale, contrasting with the rich auburn hair hanging wildly around her. Her blue eyes stared up at him as her whole body shook from panting. Below the skirt of her tattered dress were the blue shoes, the first shoes the elves had finished.

"Hello?" he said, not knowing what else to say.

She burst from the corner, rushing past as a blur of auburn and white. Once he regained his balance, he trundled up the stairs after her. She could be a thief, or a poor waif hiding in the shop. Whichever it was, she had driven the elves away. He had to stop her, find out what she had seen.

She sprinted toward the counter.

"Wait!" he said.

She turned, her hip bumping the counter. The ceramic flower pot tottered on the edge before crashing to the ground. The pot shattered and dirt flew up in a cloud.

Peter ran to the pile of dirt and searched for his flower. He should not care so much about a plant, but it had made his loneliness easier these past few months. If the roots were still intact, and there was enough soil, he could salvage it. However, as he sifted through the dirt, he couldn't even find a petal.

The girl dropped to the ground, letting out a whimper. She huddled, shivering as tears formed in her eyes. Peter rested on his knees as he stared at her. She seemed familiar. He tried to remember where they had met, yet such a memory should have been easy to find. Even Adeline Winkleston was plain beside this young woman's beauty.

"No harm's been done, as far as I can tell," he said. "I'll let you go home tonight without calling the coppers. It'll be all right."

She looked up at him, her lips quivering, her eyes pleading. Peter walked over and held out his hand when she burst into loud sobs. Scratching his head, Peter dropped onto a stool. He glanced down at his clothes. Pulling at his nightshirt, he tried to cover his legs. It would be poor for his reputation if anyone caught him alone with her. She needed to go home.

"I'll go get dressed, and then walk you home myself," he said. "Would that be better?"

She let out another whimper as more tears came.

"Would you like… er… some water?"

She seemed not to hear. Not knowing what else to do, he went to the kitchen and brought back a towel and glass of water. She gulped the water down and then wiped her face.

Once she seemed to calm, Peter said, "What's your name, miss?"

Her large blue eyes were full of sorrow as she looked at him. She pressed a hand to her throat and made a waving gesture next to her mouth.

"Sore throat?"

She shook her head before rolling to her feet and walking to the counter. Without searching, she pulled out a sketch pad and pencil. Peter frowned. She wrote on the paper and then showed it to him. His brow furrowed as he read: *me flour.*

He knew that poor chicken-scratch. That was the elves' handwriting. He looked at her. "Flour?" He pulled at his ear, deciding not to mention how odd the name was. "Were you sent by the elves?"

She shook her head, her eyes worried and her cheeks sucking in. She tapped the pencil on her chin before drawing a rough picture of a flower in a pot. She circled it and pointed at the picture and then back at herself. Peter's frown deepened. The girl sighed and drew a wobbling moon, then a stick-figure of a girl standing next to a flower pot. She added a sun next to the flower. Peter searched the picture for meaning, but a blankness clouded his mind.

She held up a finger before gliding to one of the stools, her small feet seeming to float over the ground. Her arms arched like a ballerina's. She leapt as if lighter than air and landed on a stool. She held her arms over head in a circle, mimicking a flower. With an exaggerated yawn, she stretched her arms. She crouched as if sneaking and looked around the shop, and then pantomimed climbing out of something. She danced over to the counter and pretended to sew and hammer. Then, she rushed back to the stool and returned to the flower pose.

Peter sat with his head held up by his hands, his elbows on his knees. Realization was creeping in, but he did not want to admit it. He had thought it had been elves. It had always been elves.

She danced into the kitchen and pulled out one of the repaired chairs. Her threadbare skirt flowed around her as she pirouetted across the shop floor. Her arms arched with the movement of a pretend broom. She leaped and twirled to the closed window and mimicked washing it. She raised her leg, arching her foot and then pretended to sew a shoe.

Peter sat up and said, "No. It was elves. How do you explain the pastries?"

The girl raised her eyes and let out an annoyed breath. She twirled to where the night's pastries sat on the counter. Pinching her nose, she carried the plate to the kitchen. He followed her. There, she opened the window over the sink, leaned out, and whistled. Moments later, several dogs yipped outside. She tossed the pastries out, shut the window, and washed the plate.

Peter stood in the doorway, his entire body stiff. This was impossible. Everything he had thought about those shoes and the elves—he had been wrong.

"No! No! No!" he said, pressing his hands to his head as he hurried into the storefront. The girl followed him and sat lightly on a chair.

"This is no good." He paced the shop floor. "How am I going to explain you? I'm proposing to Caroline tomorrow. She's not going to accept a man who's had a girl living in his house for months. She's not going to understand. And what'll the neighbors say? This is a scandal... a terrible scandal..."

He dropped onto a stool and stared at the broken pot. "I can't have you here. Even as a flower."

The girl walked lightly over to the small pile of dirt. She took off the shoes and raised her arms. Peter held his breath, but nothing happened. Her eyes widened, her already white skin growing paler. She jumped up and down, raised and lowered her arms, but nothing happened.

"Broke the pot, broke the spell?" Peter said. He did not understand magic. Six months ago, he hadn't even believed in it. Elves were something he could accept. But, a girl who transformed into a primrose... a primrose he had talked to and shared his secrets with?

47

He forced himself to breathe, to think. Running a hand through his fine hair, he said, "How… who are you and how did you get here?"

She picked up the paper and motioned for him to follow her to the kitchen. They sat beside each other at the small table. She drew a series of trees followed by several stick figure women dancing. She let out a breath before drawing a man with a magic wand blocked by cell bars. Beside him, she drew a girl and then pointed at herself.

"You lived in a forest with a… er… prison?" Peter said.

She nodded. Her finger pressed to the picture of the prison. She then mimed unlocking a door.

"You helped this man get free?"

Another nod came. She motioned running, and then drew her and the man standing in a field. She drew a lightning shape coming from the wand, and then an arrow from the picture of herself and added a picture of a flower.

"And he turned you into a flower?" Peter frowned. "Why would you set a fellow like that free?"

Tears trickled once more down her cheeks. Peter handed her a towel, trying not to let her tears cloud his mind. With trembling hands, she drew a heart shape. She followed it with musical notes coming from her mouth, then a line from the wand to the notes, before crossing the notes out.

"The fellow took your voice?" Peter rubbed his forehead. "Not much of a gentleman."

Tears dropped from her cheek and splattered onto the table as she lowered her chin.

He coughed uncomfortably before saying, "Pardon me asking, but uh… er… how… how'd you make so many shoes?"

She walked over to the broom in the corner and whistled before tapping it with her finger. Peter nearly fell from his chair as the broom stood on its own and began sweeping the floor. The girl snapped her fingers. The broom rested against the wall.

Peter stared. He knew magic had been going on in his shop, but he had only seen the end result. To see it work on its own was almost too much.

A rooster crowed, breaking Peter's daze. The gray light of dawn peeked through the window. He had to do something before the whole city woke.

"Now that you're a girl again," he said, "Can I help you home?"

Her face scrunched up and a sob broke from her as she shook her head.

"That'll be a no, then," he muttered as he stared at her shaking shoulders. Not knowing what else to do, he patted her arm. She gripped his hand, and a ripple of warmth ran through him, igniting a tingling far more powerful than he had ever felt before. He pulled his hand away and wiped it on his shirt. All he wanted was to kiss her cheek, and tell her it was all right. However, that was improper for a girl he had just met in person.

Peter pushed away from the table and paced the kitchen.

"Nowhere to send you, and you're a fine help in the shop." As she leaned her arms on the table and rested her head against them, he said, "I am grateful to you. I do hope you know that… Without you, I don't think this shop would still be open… But…how do I explain you to my sisters… to Caroline? They don't believe in magic." He cringed. "They'll lock me away for being mad."

He rubbed his face, when an idea came to mind. Running toward the front door, he said, "Havish'll know what to do."

As he went to grab the key, the girl gave a sharp whistle. He turned, and she pointed at his clothing. Looking down, his cheeks reddened. He was still in his night clothes.

"Thanks," he said as he ran to the stairs and motioned for the girl to follow him.

As he ushered her into his parent's old room, he said, "Keep away from the window. My sisters'll be coming by to do their cleaning sometime this morning." He paused and looked

49

at her. "You'd know my sisters, wouldn't you? You could see and hear things as a flower, right?"

She nodded.

"The things I said… you know… it's just me musing on things… Nothing serious. Don't think me too foolish. I…"

He stopped and then dodged into his own room. It was strange to know a pretty girl was in the other room while he was dressing in the first clothes he grabbed. No time to think of it. Though the buttons on his shirt were crooked, he sprinted out of the shop.

Peter ran several blocks until he reached Havish's house and pounded on the door. Marjorie Havish answered the door, as big and broad as ever, her hair snarled under her night cap.

"Mr. Talbot! What can be so important that you're breakin' down our door so early? And on Sunday!"

"I've got to see Havish," he said, trying not to look as desperate as he felt. "Tell him… it's about my nighttime help. I've… caught one."

Mrs. Havish gave him a chiding glare, when Havish came stomping to the door. He frowned as he looked at Peter. "What're you doin' here so early, Talbot?"

"The… the elves, Havish… I've caught…"

Havish's eyes brightened and he grinned. "Now, that's worth gettin' up for."

Within minutes, a fully dressed Havish was running through the streets with Peter.

"What do they look like?" Havish said. "Are they funny little fellows? That's what I always picture. And how'd you catch 'em? I thought they were wily little sprites."

"Just wait," Peter said.

Once at his shop, Peter fumbled with the lock and pushed the door open. He led Havish upstairs, and opened the master bedroom door. Sitting on the edge of the bed was the girl, lovely as he remembered, staring forlornly at the closed shutter. She sat up, and looked with wide eyes at the two men.

"That's no elf," Havish said.

"Havish, this is... she is..." Peter pressed his lips together before saying, "She's my flower."

Havish's forehead wrinkled as he glared at Peter. "I thought you were courtin' that bakery girl."

"No... I..." Peter rubbed his head. "That's not what I meant..." He sighed. "It wasn't elves. It was her..."

"You've been keepin' strange girls locked up in your shop?"

"No! It's not..." He groaned. "You remember the primrose, the one I've had sitting on my counter?"

Peter repeated the night's events, still hardly believing them himself. Maybe he shouldn't have gotten Havish. Maybe he should have let this remain secret. Yet, he still did not know what to do.

Once Peter finished, Havish kept his broad hands on his hips as he watched the girl. She kept her knees pulled to her chest, her head lowered.

"She's an unnatural sort of beauty," Havish muttered as he scratched his whiskery chin. "Fix me some breakfast, and we'll work on a plan. I think better on a full stomach."

Peter, Havish, and the girl went to the kitchen. Peter somehow kept from burning things as he made eggs and toast for the three of them. They sat at the table, Peter or Havish about to say an idea, but pausing as a problem stopped their words.

Finally, Havish jumped up, nearly knocking over the table. He held his brawny arms out and said, "Talbot, let me present to you my cousin, Flora Primrose. Poor girl. A mute whose family died from the flu. One of my other cousins sent her my way 'cause I live in a big city, and there'd be opportunity for a girl like her."

"Won't your wife see through it?"

"She's always complained I have new cousins every week that turn up askin' for a job. Most of them are related, distantly.

We'll have to forge a letter from Bruce Primrose, her uncle in a small farm town. We'll sneak her out to the Craggsville Station tonight, and she can ride in to the Pippington Station near mornin'. I'll pick her up, tellin' folks 'bout the letter she sent me. I don't have any good work for a girl like her. That'll be an excuse to take her up here and see if you've got any work. Then, we'll be able to get her into the boardin' house…"

"And get her some tutoring so she can write," Peter said with a grin. The plan could work.

A loud knocking pounded on the front door followed by Mary yelling, "Peter! Open up! It may be Sunday, but you should be up! And, I've got a surprise."

"Please, no more surprises," Peter muttered.

"Up to the room," Havish whispered. "Come along, Miss Primrose. Don't want to ruin things before we begin."

Havish pounded up the stairs behind Flora, covering the sound of her dainty feet. Peter hurried for his keys as Mary kept knocking and shouting. He tried to smile once he got the door open. However, standing beside Mary was Caroline. Mary wore a clever smirk as Caroline smiled shyly.

"Thought I'd show Caroline around," Mary said. "In case there are any… announcements tonight."

"Right, of course," Peter muttered, ushering them in quickly.

Seeing the small pile of dirt on the floor, Mary said, "Really, Peter! You've been so clean lately."

"Your flower, Peter," Caroline said. "Where is the lovely thing?"

"Knocked… I… yes, I knocked it over this morning," Peter said. "Ruined it. Had to throw it out."

"For being so successful, you are very clumsy," Mary said.

The women began chattering away as they swept and cleaned. Then, Havish came down the stairs.

"Oh, the ladies have come?" he said with a roguish grin. "Don't let 'em upstairs. They'll see the surprise you've been preparin'. It's mighty nice, Talbot. Mighty nice. I give my approval."

Mary and Caroline began chittering excitedly. Peter stared helplessly at Havish, feeling as if trapped in a vice.

"Got to be off. I'll see ya in the mornin' for business," Havish said as he dashed out the door.

Peter stared after him, his legs shaking now that he was left alone with Caroline and Mary. His quivering grew worse as Mary sent Caroline on her way and Mary came to Peter, her face bright with excitement.

"What's the surprise, Peter? Is it what I think it is? Is it upstairs? You know, if you marry Caroline, your little closet won't do at all. It's too small even for you! While I'm here, let me look at the master bedroom. Then, we can start buying new furniture. You are a wealthy shop keeper now. No need to be stingy."

She began to walk up the stairs. Peter ran after her, saying, "I've been working on it. It's not ready yet. I want it to be a surprise, Mary."

His heart quickened as she walked boldly toward the door. He leaped forward, and planted himself across it. Trying to smile, he said, "Would you like to see the ring, Mary?"

"Oh, yes, of course," she said.

He led her to his room, his breathing a little easier, and pulled out the box. She admired the plain diamond ring, cooing despite the hint of envy in her eyes.

"For how wealthy you've become, Peter, I thought this would be far fancier," Mary said.

"I- I thought... Caroline's a simple sort of girl, so a simple sort of ring..."

"Well, I suppose it will have to do," Mary sighed, handing it back to him. "Now, I think the master bedroom needs a woman's eye."

"Your old room's been fixed up," he said, jumping across the hall and throwing open the door. "Still have a bit of work to do, but it's mightily improved, don't you think?"

"You're so jittery today, Peter," she said. "Albert was just as nervous when he proposed to me. He stuttered for five minutes, and I finally had to just say, 'Yes, I'll marry you.' His eyes were so large, and he was so relieved. Try to calm yourself."

She turned back to the master bedroom. Before he could do anything, she opened the door. She let out a great cry, and Peter crumpled to the floor. Leaning his head against the wall with his eyes shut, he wondered if he could just disappear. He cringed, waiting for the slap, the shame, the loss of Caroline, the ruin of his shop.

"This is lovely! I haven't seen it this clean since Mother died," Mary said.

Peter opened his eyes slowly, wondering if he were in a dream. Though his legs still shook, he rose and approached the door. The room was dust free and appeared brighter than he remembered. There was no sign of Flora, as if she had disappeared into thin air. He found himself more worried about her disappearance than he was happy Mary had not seen her.

"The dressers will do," Mary said, scoping the room. "But this bed is so old. I think Albert and I will take it off your hands." She continued rambling through other improvements to be made. Peter remained in the doorway, seeking any sign of Flora.

Mary laid out his outfit for the evening, and left. As soon as he locked the shop door, Peter ran up the stairs and opened the bedroom door. Flora stepped meekly out of the closet, looking hopefully to him.

"Excellent job," he said, letting out a breath. "Excellent... er... you'd better stay up here for the rest of the day, if you don't mind. I'll bring you a good lunch and dinner... You don't eat dirt and water cause you were a flower for so long, do you?"

She shook her head, giving him a broad, grateful smile. A dizziness filled his head. It was probably his nerves getting the better of him. He needed to keep his mind focused. There was a proposal to prepare for.

The rest of the day was spent telling Flora about his plans for the proposal and asking her yes or no questions for advice. It was nice to have a feminine opinion without the lecturing of his sisters. He talked about his hopes of opening a second shop in North Town. It would be a better location for the wealthier customers, and give the less-wealthy folks a chance to buy new work boots. He spoke of his hopes of a family and children, of raising sons to be shoemakers, or even bankers, or lawyers, or politicians. He spoke of his worries for his nieces, being raised by his overbearing sisters. He found himself talking on and on, as if she were an old friend, as if she were an old shoe, worn in and comfortable.

He broke off the conversation to return to his room and put on his suit, vest, and top hat. Finding himself sweating from everywhere he could sweat from, he set off to the dining room at the Gormand. He ran his speech through his mind again and again. His only relief was in knowing Mr. Durbin, without prompting, had given his approval for the match a few weeks before.

At dinner, everyone crowded at the table, eating the fine goose and stuffing, the mashed potatoes, the pies. The room was vibrant with talking, laughter, and children running. Yet, Peter kept looking toward the door, wishing Flora could come. Without her help in the shop, he would not be here tonight. Bringing her, however, would also mean explaining everything.

The evening wore into a series of drinks and toasts. Charlie even stood up, at last thanking Peter for his generosity. The hour grew late, and fatigue began to overtake frivolity. Peter ran his thumb along the ring box hidden in his pocket as Caroline gave him expectant, encouraging smiles.

Pressing a hand to the table to steady himself, he rose. His feet seemed made of the jelly he had just eaten. Silence overtook the room, and all eyes were on their host, everyone smiling and knowing the outcome of his speech. Caroline arranged her curls as she looked up at him.

"Business has been good for a while now," Peter said. "And... and it seems to be steady. I... er... I'd like to thank my employees for being so hardworking and... um... I've got a bit of an announcement for you..."

Peter's mouth was dry and his words lost. Trying to find his way back to what he meant to say, he went on, "I've been thinking of opening a second shop in North Town."

The announcement was met with a round of half-hearted cheering. Charlie and Caleb were the only ones whooping vigorously.

Peter wiped some of the sweat off his brow, trying to remember what else he wanted to say. There was a reason he came here, and it was important. He began to sit down, hoping they were satisfied. His sisters glared at him, and Caroline's face drooped. He was about to settle in his chair, when Mary hissed, "Did you leave it at home? I'll go get it."

"What?" he said blankly.

"Don't you have something to say to Miss Durbin?" Molly whispered loudly.

Peter's face reddened as he put his hand in his pocket. The ring. Caroline. He turned to her. She was a sweet lady. He had thought this out. Now was the moment, but his tongue was stiff and unusable.

He forced his knee to bend and opened the box. He was unable to look at Caroline as he said, "Caroline, you're a nice girl and... any fellow would be proud to... er... I mean... you're a fine woman, and... I like you, and I think... well... you do make good pies... there's more to you than that... you're a solid sort of girl, the kind a man can rely on... so... I was wondering... if... if you wouldn't mind too much... if I... er..."

"Do say yes," Mary said, leaning excitedly over the table.

"I couldn't ask for a lovelier girl for a sister-in-law," Molly said.

"I... er..." Peter tried to push out the words, but they would not come.

56

Caroline placed her hands around his. She leaned close with an eager smile, and said, "Nothing would make me happier than to be your wife, Peter Talbot."

She kissed him, and he stared, frozen in place until his sisters prodded him. He fumbled with the ring and placed it on Caroline's finger. She looked at it, giving a happy, contented sigh before throwing her arms around him. Peter's breath became shallow, as if he were being enclosed in a box.

Peter's feet led the way home as his mind hazed over. He arrived at his door, not sure how he had gotten there. With a sigh, he unlocked the door and stepped inside the sane space of his shop. He dropped his keys as Flora appeared.

He pressed against the door as she flitted through the shop, gesturing at where she had swept and what she had cleaned. She twirled to the counter and showed him the shoes she had completed in his absence. He smiled, warmed by her youthful excitement. Then, his dinner threatened to revisit him as he realized his sisters or Caroline could walk in at any moment.

Taking off his hat, he said, "I'm an engaged man now."

She stopped, drooping like a balloon suddenly deflated. Her eyes became large, filling quickly with tears. She attempted to smile before flinging her arms in a graceful arc and leaping up the stairs. Peter's eyes followed her, his heartbeat quickening. He wanted to follow her, but he was better than that. He was engaged to Caroline. There would be no thinking of any other girl. Not in such a way.

☐

Chapter 5

A few hours before dawn, Peter stood at the Craggsville station and handed the train ticket to Flora. She huddled in his mother's old dress and faded hat. It bagged around her, but was better than the rags she had been wearing. She gripped his arm and shook her head as he went to leave.

Gently pulling her hand away, he said, "It'll be all right. Havish'll bring you to the shop in no time."

On his way to his delivery truck, he paused to look back. She hid in the shadow of a tree, clutching the old dress around her. Perhaps he should stay a bit and make her feel safer. He flexed his fingers and kept walking. She would be back and safe in no time.

Once returned home, he busied his hands and mind with work on shoes. An hour before the store opened, he decided it was best to keep to usual habits. He straightened his coat, pulled on his hat and took his daily walk to the bakery.

Inside, Caroline was surrounded by a crowd of women. All of them chattered as she held out her hand, displaying her fine ring. Peter's stomach churned. Hopefully, being married would help him understand women.

Upon seeing Peter, Caroline let out a gleeful cry. She bobbed around the counter and threw her arms around him. He fell against the wall, grasping the door frame to keep on his feet. She kissed him on the cheek and then returned to her place behind the counter. Peter adjusted his hat, trying not to be aware of the knowing smiles from female customers.

Caroline held out two boxes of pastries and said, "Papa says they're free for future sons-in-law."

"Please," Peter said. "Let me pay. I'd feel—"

"None of that now." Mr. Durbin popped his head out of the kitchen. "You're nearly family, Mr. Talbot. No need to be shy."

"I... er... only need one box," he said, remembering the sour look on Flora's face. "Please."

Caroline pushed the boxes into his arms. Peter walked back to his shop slowly, wishing he had been able to pay for them. Then, maybe, the boxes wouldn't feel so heavy.

Just after he set the boxes down on the shop counter, Havish arrived with Flora. She wore a dress borrowed from one of Havish's daughters, the sleeves bunched and the skirt too long.

"My boys at the workshop tried to convince me she'd do well there," Havish said. "May have to steal her away, if you don't treat her right. No one's asked any odd questions yet. My wife even took the whole story without raising an eyebrow. She just cried over the poor girl, gave her one of Evelyn's old dresses, and sent her on her way."

Flora beamed at Peter, twirling to show the dress. He nodded at her and returned a squeamish smile. He doubted his sisters would accept her so easily.

"Made an extra workstation for you downstairs," he said. "And a list of work. You've seen how the shop runs. Can't do it the same as when you're by yourself at night. No magic, Miss Flora. The boys'll realize something's up. If you don't think enough's been done, go ahead and take some shoes home."

Then to Havish, he said, "Do you have any immediate appointments?"

"Everythin' can be pushed back if I get to spend time with this lovely girl."

Peter nodded, trying to think. He pulled out a money pouch he had prepared earlier. "Take her to Chancey's for a few dresses to be made. Tell him the whole story, especially if Molly is nearby. That'll be enough for all the town to know it. Say the money's a loan from you, to get your cousin started."

59

"Talbot, you may become as devious as I am," Havish said with a grin. "And, I'll get the boardin' house and tutor set up this mornin' too. She'll be back before ten."

Charlie, Caleb, William, and the three new employees came in and set to work as usual. Peter pulled William aside and explained they were getting a new employee, a young lady. The store opened, and a few orders came in. As usual, there was more work than they could reasonably do. Servants arrived from North Town, delivering orders with deposits.

Charlie and Peter loaded the finished shoes in the delivery truck Peter. Charlie turned the crank, and the engine puttered to life. The purr of the motor still surprised Peter. He climbed in the driver's seat and moved to push on the throttle, when Havish returned with Flora. She grinned as she held the skirt of her new dress around her and swooshed it playfully. She waved at Peter and he let out a laugh before waving back.

"Well, here she is," Havish shouted over the engine. "Chancey had this one on a shelf and said it'd do better for her."

Charlie grinned as he leaned against the truck. "Havish, who is this lovely girl?"

"Cousin of mine," Havish said. "Miss Flora Primrose. Sweet lady. Talbot here's given her a job at the shop. Turns out she's an excellent shoemaker."

Charlie's grin broadened. He tucked his thumbs into his belt loops and puffed up his chest. "Seems excellent. If you don't mind, Mr. Talbot, I'll show her around the shop for you."

"William can do it," Peter said. "We need to deliver shoes."

"Good to meet you, Miss Primrose," Charlie said with a tip of his cap. "If you need anything, let me know."

Peter pushed on the throttle. With each delivery, he wondered if Flora was settling in well, if the other workers were welcoming her, or if she was having trouble.

Around noon, he and Charlie returned to the shop. As they drove past, a crowd of men pushed against each other to get inside. Peter hopped out and Charlie parked the truck in the alleyway

"Excuse me. Pardon me," Peter said as he pushed through the jostling crowd. He had gotten used to the crowd of women pushing in, but had never seen men so excited for shoes.

Coming around the main counter, Peter found William cowering in the corner, his hands on his graying head. Peter glanced out. At the center of the crowd of men, Flora smiled sweetly as she worked on cutting leather. Each movement was one of a continual dance, her mind and body focused on her work, unaware of the salivating men surrounding her.

A feeling Peter hardly recognized burned in his breast. Flora was a lady, and deserved better than this. Before his plan was clear, he pushed his way to the center of the crowd. A few men tried to block his path, but he slipped around them and at last reached Flora's side.

Her face lit up as she noticed Peter. She picked up a pair of shoes and proudly displayed her finished work.

"I see," he muttered. "Well done..."

He looked out at the sea of men encircling him. Many were at least a head taller than him. Yet, this was his shop, and Flora his employee and friend. Trying to hide the quivering of his legs, he stepped onto a stool.

"Gentlemen," he said loudly. "If you would please... If you're here to buy shoes, make an appointment. If not, I'll ask you... you to carry on... please."

Flora started back, just now seeing the wall of men. The men remained, oblivious of Peter. Fear crept into her face as she pressed against Peter's side. He put a hand on her shoulder, partially to comfort, partially to steady himself.

"I..." He swallowed as his jaw tightened. This gawking and grinning was not how a man should treat a lady, especially one as sweet as Flora. He tugged his vest and shouted, "We are closing for lunch!"

William broke from his daze and helped Peter push the men out the front door. Men shouted, and a few swung for Peter as they pressed against him. Peter barely ducked in time, and then dodged behind the counter. Sitting on the shelf was a bag of smoke snaps from Rompell's last visit. Peter grabbed a few and tossed them into the shop. Blue and red smoke billowed up, sparks glittering in the haze. Men cried out, pressed toward the door, and ran into the street.

As the haze cleared, William leaned against the door to hold back the onslaught of men, and Peter turned the key.

Letting out a breath, William whispered, "You've got to fire her, Mr. Talbot. I moved her up here because the other men couldn't get any work done with her down in the workshop. They just stared at her. Then, all those men came in. Only one or two pretended to be interested in shoes. Pretty girls like that are bad for business, Mr. Talbot."

"I can't fire her," Peter said. "I promised Havish I'd give her a job. She's got nowhere else to go."

"Maybe she could work in your sister's dress shop, or your other sister's hat shop? Just not here, Mr. Talbot."

"She stays, William."

"I don't like it, sir."

They both jumped as someone pounded on the door. Peter glanced, and there stood a smiling Caroline carrying a lunch basket. She waved shyly at him. Peter tried to smile back as he let her inside. She giggled before kissing his cheek.

"There are some very unhappy men out there," she said, taking his arm and leading Peter toward the kitchen. She stopped as her eyes met Flora's. Flora's face was pale, her eyes large and round.

Peter shuddered as he noticed Caroline's expression. He had seen such a look on a cat when another one tried to steal its dinner. He had never expected something so vicious to be on Caroline's sweet face.

"Er... let me introduce... this is one of Havish's cousins, Miss Flora Primrose. She's an expert shoemaker, so Havish asked me to give her a job," Peter said. "She's a good worker."

He paused. "Uh… Miss Flora, this is… er… my… fiancée, Caroline."

Flora gave a weak smile and polite curtsy. Caroline returned a stiff nod.

Peter took her arm and said, "Um… er… what'd you bring for lunch today?"

Caroline was civil during the meal, but kept the conversation short. Peter spent most of the meal fumbling with his utensils, trying to focus just on eating.

Peter escorted her to the door and reopened for business. During the afternoon, male servants dropped off orders, and lingered by the counter where Flora worked. Peter shooed them away as quickly as he could, trying to stem off another incoming flood of gawkers. Charlie spent most of his day finding odd jobs to do on the main floor. He leaned on a broom, talking and boasting, trying to start a conversation. She kept her focus on the shoes, her hands trembling under the gaze of strangers.

The day was finally coming to a close, when Rompell entered.

"My housekeeper's been wearing broken shoes for days," he said as he held out a woman's shoe with a broken heel. "Had to steal it from her and…"

His voice trailed off as Flora came up from the workshop. She went to walk over to Peter, when she saw Rompell. She stepped back, her shoulders trembling, all color gone from her face.

Rompell touched his hand to his forehead and bowed in a Sandarian greeting. "Good evening. I am Rompell of Sandar."

"This is my new worker, Miss Flora Primrose," Peter said, trying not to frown.

"Miss Primrose?" Rompell tilted his head and glanced at the counter where Flora had sat in flower form for so many months. He rubbed his chin as he raised his eyebrows. "Interesting."

He moved toward her, but she stepped back behind a stool.

"No need to worry, Miss Flora. Rompell here's an old customer of mine, and a good sort."

Rompell waved his hand. "I have done many things in my past to frighten others. May I ask, miss, what I have done to you?"

Flora's mouth tightened and she shook her head.

"She's got no voice," Peter said. Perhaps Rompell could explain a few things. "You've met before?"

"I would remember meeting such a lady," Rompell said as he turned back toward Peter. He paused as he sniffed the air. A small smile formed. "Mr. Talbot, why have you been setting off my smoke snaps in your shop?"

"Oh, um…" Peter rubbed his hand on his vest. "We had a bit too much of a crowd earlier, and… um… needed to clear things out a bit."

Rompell laughed and reached into his pocket. He dropped a small canvas bag on the counter. "Here are a few more, if you need them."

Peter tried to laugh in return, but it only came out as an awkward huff.

Leaning over the counter, Rompell whispered, "Take good care of the lady. I am sure she is more than she seems."

Peter frowned as Rompell left some money on the counter and then stepped outside.

As they closed up shop, Flora seemed to calm, and returned to flitting across the floor. Peter watched her, wondering what Rompell suspected, and if the man knew of or believed in magic. He had always thought the smoke snaps were a few chemicals mixed together to let off the appearance of magic. He stared down at the bag, wondering if there was more to it.

At the close of the day, Peter walked Flora to the boarding house. A few men lingered and grinned at her, but Peter sent them a sharp glare.

"Tomorrow will be better," he said as he left her on the doorstep. She gave him a warm smile and squeezed his hand before disappearing inside.

When he returned to the shop, he found himself staring at the spot she had stood for so long. She needed a job, and he needed her help. However, no one should be gawked at all day. There had to be something he could do.

As he wandered upstairs later, he stopped at the spare room. He opened the door. She could work here, away from the eyes of men, and she could use her magic. Perhaps it would be lonely, but she could come downstairs whenever she wanted. And, it would keep her from those who might discover her secret. Yes. That was the best plan.

Chapter 6

The plan worked over the next few months as the winter frost passed through the town. Peter found himself looking forward to Flora's smiling face as she came dancing in every morning. She often showed him her work from the tutor. Her writing was becoming more legible and her spelling vastly improving. Charlie always arrived soon after. He chattered nervously while helping her gather the day's supplies and carry them upstairs. Once the door closed and the shop opened, Flora would set to work alone, able to use her magic in secret.

Now and then, she would come sweeping down the stairs. The men in the shop would gape, forgetting the women beside them. Flora would dance across the room in her beautiful, odd fashion, retrieve what she had come for, smile at Peter, and then float up the stairs. Even after she disappeared, the men would continue staring. Their female companions would then shout at them, and the men returned to the present moment.

Caroline did not say much of Flora, except to glare every time Flora appeared. Peter never really understood this. Flora was a nice, lovely girl. Eventually, Caroline would take to Flora and her sweet innocence. Peter just needed to be patient.

Peter watched the days passing on the calendar, waiting for the day he and Caroline would marry. Though the wedding was set for early summer, Peter debated pushing it back. The shop was so busy now, he had no time to think of the ceremony.

Spring arrived at last with blue skies, cool breezes, and bright flowers on windowsills and in the park. One day, Flora came in happily, a wreath of bright marigolds on her head, and a pot of white and yellow daisies under her arm. She twirled through the shop, setting the flowers on the counter, and leaping to some unheard music. Upon seeing Peter's confused expression, she wrote on a slate, "The first flowers of spring."

She grinned before pirouetting over to the pot of daisies and drinking in the fragrance. Charlie crept in through the front door. With a smirk, he stood behind Flora, leaned toward her, and shouted, "Boo!"

Flora's eyes went wide and she grabbed the counter to stop her fall. Charlie gripped his chest as he laughed heartily.

"Morning, Miss Flora," he said as he calmed himself and smoothed his hair. "You're a lovely girl, you know." He gave her a broad grin as he leaned against the counter. "And spring in Pippington is a lovely season. I've been thinking, it'd be nice if you'd go for a stroll with me on Saturday." He gestured at the pot of flowers. "Brinfir park's full of flowers this time of year. I can show you around. It'll be a grand old day. Do you want to come?"

Tilting her head, Flora looked to Peter as if asking permission.

"There's nothing wrong in going for a stroll with a young man," Peter said, giving her a gentle smile. "Charlie's a good fellow. It'd probably be nice."

Her eyes lowered, her face somber a moment. She took in a breath before giving a half-hearted smile and nodding to Charlie. The young man beamed as he grabbed Flora's hand and shook it with vigor.

"Thank you, Miss Flora. I'm so... It'll be lovely. Just lovely."

Charlie seemed to work twice as fast as usual for the rest of the day. Peter set to the day's business, deciding Flora was good for the boy. Charlie had matured much over the last few months, and was fast becoming an industrious, driven man. Perhaps, he would be good for Flora too.

On Friday, Charlie came to Peter and said, "I don't know what to do tomorrow. A walk just don't seem enough to charm

Miss Flora... I'm likely to make a fool of myself. You've got a steady girl, Mr. Talbot. What do you think I should do?"

Peter tapped his fingers on the counter. He said, "Caroline and I are going on a picnic tomorrow around eleven. You can meet us at the red gazebo in Brinfer Park, and I can do my best to help."

Charlie grinned. "Thank you, sir. I'll see you there."

The next morning, Peter bought extra food for the picnic and packed the basket. At ten, he picked up Caroline from her house. She wore a pleasant forest-green dress that she believed complemented her brown eyes, and a bonnet with false flowers on it. She smiled brightly as she set her arm in his and they walked toward the park. She talked of the wedding and of the little improvements she would make to the shop afterward.

As they neared the park, the conversation lulled. Peter rubbed his thumb on his lapel before saying, "Oh, I probably should mention... Charlie asked Miss Flora to go for a stroll today."

"Oh," Caroline said, her cheeks taut. "How good of him."

"He's been coming in early just to gander at her for months now."

"Him and every other male in town," Caroline said.

Peter frowned. "She can't help that." They walked a few steps before he said, "Well, Charlie was nervous, so I invited them to join us for our picnic."

Caroline let go of his arm. Peter grimaced as her eyes flashed wide. "You invited Flora Primrose on our picnic?"

Peter pulled off his hat and rubbed his head. "I invited Charlie, so he'd have a more comfortable setting with Miss Flora. He thought that, well, since I'd been able to... you know... gain your... heart that... um... I'd be able to give him some... romantic advice. I'm just trying to help."

"He came to you for advice on romance?"

Peter raised his eyebrows. "We're engaged... aren't we?"

Her mouth became small and tight. Peter held the basket between them, hoping it might protect him from any oncoming storms.

"Peter, you know I care for you, but, if it weren't for your sisters' prodding," she said, "I do not know if you would ever have asked me to dinner."

A pain stung in Peter's chest. "Every fellow needs a little help, I suppose... And Charlie... He's grown into a decent young man, and I think Miss Flora would do well by him. If he stays with the shop, he'll have a steady career. Really, he'd be better for her than all the fancy men who hang around to stare at her. I'm just trying to be a good friend to Charlie and Miss Flora. Do as any good friend would do."

"She is not your friend, Peter," Caroline said. "She is your employee. What do you think others will say when they see a successful business owner, and an engaged man, fraternizing with a shop girl?"

Peter's brow furrowed. "They're both my employees. My father took his workers out for dinner or a drink now and then. I don't see any impropriety, Caroline."

"You see nothing wrong with having Miss Flora Primrose flitting about your shop?"

"No. She's a nice girl, and a good worker. Having her around seems to brighten the place."

"This is what troubles me, Peter." Caroline let out a sigh before holding out her arm for him to take. "But, you have made a promise, haven't you?"

She kept her arm stiff as they walked to her park. Her eyes remained focused straight ahead, and there was no more conversation. Peter was moderately relieved as he saw Charlie walking toward the red gazebo. Flora was frolicking in the nearby field, her arms arching as she tried to take everything in. Her sky-blue dress floated around her, even as sensible older women stared and whispered to each other behind fans. Then, Flora cartwheeled, her skirt flying up. Caroline let out a grunt of disgust. Peter winced. He would have to pull Flora aside and talk a bit about propriety.

Upon seeing Peter, Charlie waved and yelled a hello. Peter gave a polite smile and wave in return. Flora's cheeks were pink from exercise as she waved at Peter and ran to join Charlie. The sun shone on her hair, picking up the red highlights and illuminating the wreath of white flowers encircling her head.

Within minutes, Peter and Charlie set out a blanket on a hill overlooking the pond. Sandwiches were made and distributed in silence. Soon, Charlie filled the quiet with boasts and stories, his chatter rapid and nervous. Caroline sat stiffly, her legs properly to the side, while Flora sat cross-legged like a child, her skirt stretched over her knees. Peter found himself looking at her feet shod in the delicate blue shoes that had started his good fortune. He noted the smooth arch, the round heel, how lovely the shoe complimented the shape of her foot.

His eyes turned to Caroline's sturdy black shoes, with the small heel, and the generic toe. The footwear was stiff and firm. He had offered to make her new ones, but she insisted she was a humble girl and did not want to put on airs.

Charlie was in the middle of a sentence, when Flora cupped her hands over her mouth. She blew into them, and a strange honking sound came out. Both Charlie and Caroline cried out as a swan landed on the middle of the blanket. It lowered its head, bending its neck, and stretching out a wing as if bowing to Flora. She folded one arm like a wing, held out the other and mimicked the bow.

Using her tongue and lips to make noise, Flora clicked at it. The swan clicked its beak, honked, and made a strange purr in reply. Flora's eyes lit up and she grinned. She clicked at it some more, and the swan let out a friendly purring sound before bowing its head and leaving. Flora leapt to her feet and bounded down the hill, rapidly picking up speed. Too stunned to move, Caroline, Charlie and Peter watched. The momentum was more than she counted on as she reached the bottom. She tripped over the bank and flew into the pond.

Peter was on his feet before he realized he was moving.

"That girl may be a danger to society," Caroline said as Peter and Charlie hurried down the hill.

Urging speed while trying not to tumble, Peter hoped she would not drown. Flora splashed in the water, her dress caught on the reeds. Charlie threw off his boots before stepping into the mossy pond, grimacing as the mud squished between his toes. Peter hesitated on the shore as Charlie helped Flora pull her skirt from the reeds. As they moved toward the bank, Peter held out his arms. Just as Charlie caught hold, he slipped in the mud. Panic cut off Peter's breath as he rushed toward the water. He splashed and kicked until he was able to find footing and stand. Charlie grabbed his arm and tried to pull him on shore, when Charlie slipped and fell into the water again. Flora sat laughing silently on the bank, her hair hanging wet around her. Her dress clung to her, accentuating her slight body and feminine curves. Charlie and Peter slogged to the shore. Once on land, Charlie and Peter laughed as they fell onto the grass.

"Really, Peter." Caroline stood over them.

Peter tried to stop laughing as he rose. His boots squelched with water as he moved to Caroline's side.

"Charlie, you should probably walk Miss Flora home," Caroline said. "I doubt she wishes to catch cold."

Flora ran to Peter's side and tugged on his arm. Quickly, she raised one arm, pantomiming a tree, and mimicked dancing with her other hand. She then pointed at the water and motioned swimming. She dropped her arms as she saw Caroline's glare.

Peter pressed a hand to Flora's shoulder. "It's been a lovely afternoon, Miss Flora. You should probably head home with Charlie."

Flora's eyes pleaded with him, seeking for him to understand something. Even if he had paper and a pen, the paper would be too wet to use.

"Tell me later, all right?" he said.

"Come along, Miss Flora," Charlie said, holding his hand out to her. She looked at his hand before giving him a tense smile and taking it. "Thank you, Mr. Talbot. It's been a lovely day."

Peter could feel Flora's eyes following him as he led Caroline up the hill. Neither he or his fiancé spoke as they cleaned up the remains of the picnic.

He was folding up the blanket, when Caroline said, "When I am Mrs. Talbot, I expect my husband to act with more dignity and discretion than has been shown today."

"It was all an accident," Peter said as he placed the blanket in the basket.

"You have every right to fire her for her behavior today," she said. "Exposing her undergarments in public! Making a fool of herself, and you."

"She's from a small town," he said. "She's an innocent, naïve girl. Maybe... maybe you can help her... teach her to be a lady, like you."

"That is Mr. Havish's trouble," she said. "Not yours, Peter. She is his cousin, and his concern. She is not worth the scandal today might bring."

"She's been through a lot," Peter said. "Lost everything. She's got no one but me to look after her."

"And why is that? Why do you feel so responsible for her? She has Mr. Havish. She does not need you."

He put on his hat, wondering what to answer. He would have to tell Caroline the truth someday, but now did not seem the right time.

"I can't explain it all, but..." He glanced out. Flora and Charlie were disappearing around a corner. "She's no relation to Havish or me... She... just showed up on my doorstep a while back, lost and confused... You see, some man, some sorcerer tricked her into falling in love with him. She set the evil man free, and he cursed her, making her lose her voice..."

He paused. Caroline's frown proved she already doubted the tale. He sighed. Perhaps the truth was what she needed.

"The man, he turned her into a flower... you remember the primrose that you complemented so much, the one sitting on my counter for months... it was her, but I didn't know. One night I discovered her... accidentally broke the spell... She had nowhere to go, for who would believe such a story? And, she has no voice to explain herself. Havish just said she was his cousin to help cover things up..."

"Did Havish help you come up with this preposterous story?" Caroline said, her face turning red. "Or did she bewitch you? What makes you think I would believe a word of that? Even one word! I am not some naïve girl you can make such lies to, Peter Talbot."

She began to turn away, but stopped. "I know you're a steady man, so I'll give you a chance to prove yourself: Get rid of her. I will have no word of her in the future, and I do not want to see her again. Do whatever you must, but I will not marry you if you keep her in your shop."

Peter stepped toward her. "Caroline, please. Go ask Mr. Havish. We can go right now. He'll confirm everything."

"Would you choose this waif over your fiancée, Peter?"

"She is just an innocent..."

"How can you tell me that? I am sure you have noticed how she looks at you with her large blue eyes. She worships you, Peter, more than a single girl should care for a soon-to-be-married man. I said nothing because I want to trust you, but after today... After today, I cannot be sure of you."

"Caroline... I..." He stopped, unsure what to say. "She doesn't look at me that way."

Caroline shot him a glare. "Good day, Mr. Talbot."

Peter stood holding the basket in his hand as Caroline stormed away. With his head throbbing and his clothes dripping, he began a lonely walk to his shop. Flowers would not be enough to heal the sudden rift between him and Miss Caroline Durbin this time.

Chapter 7

The next morning, Peter sat on the edge of his bed, his mind running through the events at the park. There may have been better things to say to Caroline. He had promised to marry Caroline, and with that came responsibilities and trust. He had to change her mind about Flora. She had to see Flora's sweetness and innocence.

He jumped as the front door rattled on its hinges. Molly shouted for him to open, but, this time, he did not run to get the door. Judging by the pounding, Caroline had already spoken with his sisters. He dug his fingers into the mattress, deciding to remain where he was. Talking to his sister now would be like jumping in a cage with a starved beast. He preferred his skin to stay on his body.

He hid in his shop until Monday morning. As he went about opening the store, he was still unsure what to do. Flora came in first, the lightness of her step gone as she went upstairs to her work bench. The time Charlie usually came passed, but William entered early.

"Mr. Talbot, can I have a word?" he said, his cap in his hand.

Peter led William into the kitchen and sat across the table from him. William frowned at the table, heavy bags under his eyes. "As you know, I worked for your father from an apprentice. I stayed on 'cause I like the regular work of making boots. Your father was a good, steady man, and I'm proud to have worked for him.

"I've been considering my stake in the shop, and looking to my future, and… it's tough to say it, sir, but I've saved up quite a bit, and found a nice shop a few blocks away. I'm going into business on my own, sir. I'll finish up the week, and finish my tasks."

Peter's lungs ached as if William had knocked the air out. Looking into William's brown eyes, he said, "You're my best worker. You're a steady, good man. If this is what you want, I'll support you, but I don't want to lose you."

"I've been thinking of it for a while, sir. Past time I moved on." William scratched his nose as he glanced out the window. "And, well, sir, there're rumors you've... I'm not much for gossip, but these rumors could be true."

Peter rubbed his temples, waiting for what he knew would come.

"It's been going round that you've..." William coughed into his hand. "Been lying to Miss Durbin and running about with Miss Flora. A few months ago, I'd back you up to any man... but... she does come in early, and in the evening you go and check on her alone... and the way she looks at you sir... Even an old bachelor like me knows those kinds of looks, Mr. Talbot."

"But, I'm not..." Peter breathed, unable to form a louder sound.

"Whether you are or not, the rumors don't shine well on me, sir. I've got my reputation to think about."

Peter's eyes stared forward, but he saw nothing.

William rose. "I'll get to my work then, sir."

"No," Peter said, forcing himself to focus. "I'll pay you a week's wages, and a bit extra. You've worked here long enough to earn that. If you've got plans for your own shop, you'll just be wasting your time here."

He walked to the safe and put the money in a pouch. Handing it to William, he said, "It's been an honor to work with you."

William grunted with a nod before walking out the door.

Peter stared after his longtime worker, hardly aware as Havish came in with a pile of leather. Dropping the load on the counter, Havish said, "What were you bloomin' thinking, telling Miss Durbin the truth? I'd not have told my own wife even if I was threatened. Rumors are buzzin' like mad. It's a mighty scandal, Talbot."

"William just quit," Peter said, still standing at the door. "He's going to open his own shop."

Havish waved his hand. "He'll be crawlin' back for a job in a month."

Peter glanced at Havish. "I'd not blame you if you refuse to sell me leather anymore. I'll find another supplier. You don't need a customer with such a reputation."

"You are one of the best men I know," Havish said. "Besides, I make enough money off your shop alone to pay most of my workers. I'll not give that up."

"I don't think business will last long."

"You'll lose the locals for a bit," Havish said, joining Peter beside the door. "But, a scandal will draw more of the rich folks. I think Cordwainer's has had rumors of three affairs since you began competing with him, and I'll tell you, he started them off. Creates interest for a bit. Makes the ladies feel a bit naughty."

"But, none of it's true," Peter said.

"True or not, it'll blow over in a month or two. Some other scandal'll take its place, and folks'll come back for Talbot's Boots. No one make shoes so well."

"William will."

"Yes, but he's not got your business savvy."

"Caroline… Miss Durbin… she told me I either have to fire Flora, or give up my engagement."

Havish was quiet a moment. "It wouldn't be too much of a loss."

"It would be a great loss," Peter said. "Flora's what has made me so successful. I'd be ungrateful to toss her out."

Havish raised an eyebrow. "I was talkin' 'bout Miss Durbin. She'll find some other steady, quiet shop owner. Men'll queue up to mend her broken heart. I've seen it dozens of times. A girl with a broken engagement is a fine prize."

"I promised to marry her."

"Do you still want to?" Havish straightened the stack of leather. "She's the one who started the rumors by talkin' to your sisters. My wife came back from the baker's this mornin', rattling off what Miss Durbin said about you, and how she's all in tears. You'll still have your work cut out for you. You could buy a large piece of jewelry, but that'll only stop the wound for a bit."

Peter raised his head and turned to Havish. "Can you find a job for Flora? Then, I can keep my promise to both of them."

Havish leaned close and whispered, "You're choosing Miss Durbin over that gorgeous girl? You are either mad or an idiot."

Peter pulled his coat straight. "I am an honorable man."

"I'll look," Havish said, pressing his finger into Peter's chest. "Cause we're in this mess together, but I don't think it's wise."

Peter paid Havish, and the tanner left. A few minutes later, Caleb entered with the three newer workers. Grinning, Caleb said, "Been rumors flying around today."

Peter glanced at Caleb, but said nothing. He just wanted to go and hide in his room. However, it was upstairs, as was Flora. What other rumors would come from that?

Caleb burst out laughing. "Funniest stuff I've ever heard. You and Miss Flora. You're the most square, honest man I've ever met. I know I've had my grudges, but I trust you, sir. I think you're just suffering from a woman's insecurities. You should hear the accusations my wife throws at me every morning. Only half of them are true."

The three other workers joined Caleb's laughter as they went down to the work room. Peter shut his eyes. His head throbbed.

"Mr. Talbot."

Peter looked up at Charlie, standing on the other side of the counter with his head lowered. He looked as miserable as William.

"Can we speak privately, sir?"

Once again, Peter was in the kitchen, sitting across from his employee.

"On Saturday, when I walked Miss Flora back to the boarding house," Charlie said. "I tried to kiss her cheek. Just an innocent peck... She jumped as if I'd thrown a snake at her, and then ran away. I didn't understand... but... then I heard the rumors goin' round."

"The rumors. Of course." Peter sighed.

Charlie ventured a glance at Peter. "I see they've reached you too. Thing is... I know you haven't done anything of the like. You wouldn't have tried to help me on Saturday, if you had... but, it got me thinkin'... I saw the look she gave you as you left with Miss Durbin. It's that look, sir. I can't compete with how she feels for you, and I can't think of breaking her heart..." He swallowed. "I passed William in the street. He offered me a job as full shoemaker in the shop he's opening. I was thinking of accepting. You see, Mr. Talbot, I can't work here anymore. Not with her around."

Peter rubbed his face before saying, "If that's what you want to do, Charlie. You're a good worker. If you ever decide to come back, I'll keep a job for you."

"Thank you, sir."

As Charlie left with his week's wages, the shop opened as usual. Peter worked in the back of the shop, avoiding the eyes of local customers walking past. He felt their glares through the window. The rich ones still came, just as Havish had said. Yet, Peter needed to find new workers. Who would work for a man with a tarnished name?

In the late morning, both Molly and Mary arrived. He shut the door of the kitchen and stood still and silent, waiting for the coming storm. Their faces were red and fuming, the shouts cutting and condescending.

"You fire that girl right now," Molly said.

"Send her packing. She's nothing to you. Certainly not worth this trouble," Mary said.

"Certainly not," Molly said. "And then you go to Miss Caroline Durbin—"

"Yes. On your knees," Mary said.

"—And you beg."

"Yes, beg. Beg for her forgiveness."

"You'll never find a better woman."

"None better. And how do you think your reputation reflects on my dear husband?"

"Our husbands' shops will be ruined."

"Just ruined."

"Our families will be thrown out on the street."

"We'll starve, and what will you do then?"

"Did you think about that when you began dallying with this girl?"

Exhausted and beaten, he hoped they were finished.

They each took a breath for another tirade, when he said, "You know I am an honest man. I have done nothing wrong."

"Honest! Honest? How dare you use such a word!"

"How can we trust a man who keeps a young woman around in secret?"

Something caved in his mind, and his patience cracked. Throwing open the kitchen door, he shouted, "Out! Both of you!"

"Now, Peter, that is no way to talk to—"

"Out!" The word was fresh and beautiful. "I am an honorable man. Out!"

"I'll send my husband to deal with you."

"You should be ashamed of yourself."

They shuffled out the door and bustled angrily down the street.

Customers were silent, staring from their places around the shop as Peter stood with his fists clenched. Color drained his face as he realized his sisters would be back, and with a worse offence.

"Pay 'em no mind, ma'am," Caleb said as he slid a shoe onto a lady's foot. "They just like making a scene."

Peter marched down to the workshop and slammed nails into shoes. He had to choose what to do, and the choice should be easy. Yet, he could not give up Flora to marry Caroline, nor could he give up Caroline to keep Flora in the shop.

Havish returned in the afternoon. Peter set down the hammer, wishing the weight in his stomach would leave.

"I found her a job at a glove maker's uptown," the tanner said. "Told him she can sew embroidery. No one down here would take her."

"Thank you," Peter said, wiping sweat from his brow. "You should go tell her."

"I mean little more than spit to her," Havish said. "It needs to come from you, Talbot."

"I can't be alone with her. I don't want any more rumors."

"Then I'll go and stand as chaperone."

Peter walked up the stairs, his shoes as heavy as boulders. He hesitated at the door of her makeshift workshop. He took a breath and stepped inside. The room was empty, her remaining work unfinished on the table. His heart pressed against his chest, aching. Had she left to avoid further shame? She could not have disappeared as quickly as she had appeared. Perhaps the swan she had talked to had carried her away.

Thumping sounded in the master bedroom. With a silent prayer, he ran to the door and threw it open. He let out a breath as he saw Flora standing on a chair, leveling curtains. The room was bright, the walls a fresh, spring-filled yellow, the bedspread new, the furniture polished.

Streaks of tears were on her face as she looked at him. She stepped down from the chair and lowered her head.

"How long have you been working on this?" he said.

Her shoulders slunk and her slender frame shivered.

"This looks lovely," he said, stepping further in. He prepared another complement, but stopped. Remembering why he came, he pulled up the other chair and motioned for her to sit.

Her hair draped over her face as she kept her head turned away. Havish quietly shut the door as he stepped outside. Peter forced his breathing to stay steady despite the rapid pounding of his heart. Sitting alone with Flora made his task harder by the moment.

"I'm sure you've heard the rumors going around," he said as he wiped his sweating hands on his pants. "Caroline told me I had to let you go, or break off the engagement. It's not been an easy decision, Miss Flora."

A sob shattered through her. Peter shifted in his chair. He wanted to put his arm around her and tell her it was all right. Gripping the seat of his chair helped stop the improper impulse.

"But, I've got to be true to my word, and I've promised myself to Caroline. Mr. Havish has found you a good job, and he'll take you there."

Her shoulders shook, her cries growing louder.

"I'm grateful for everything you've done for me, Flora," Peter said. "You're a wonderful girl, and I can't begin to say how much you've helped me and my shop." He rubbed his forehead. "There's nothing to be sad about. You'll make a good wage, and be able to keep your boarding room. If you need anything, go to Havish, and he'll let me know. I'll do everything I can to help you. I'll stop and visit, when I can. It'll be all right."

He did not feel things would be all right. His stomach was twisted in unfixable knots. Her tears caressed the contours of her face. She was as delicate now as the flower he had taken from the field. If there were going to be rumors about him, at least it was with a fine woman.

He did not want her to go.

Yet, he forced himself to stand. Trying to quiet her sobs, she stood as well. He reached out his hand. She stared at it before raising her head. Her crystal-blue eyes were so wide. Peter gasped as Flora threw her arms around him. She shook as she hugged him tightly. Her face pressed into his shoulder, her tears wetting his shirt.

Not knowing what else to do, he patted her back, and then held her. He tried to ignore the warmth filling him. All he wanted was to press his lips to her cheek and hold her, cradle her until her tears ended. He shut his eyes. He was engaged to Caroline Durbin.

Flora's hand pressed against his chest. His breath stilled. Then, she kissed his cheek. Her lips lingered as heat flooded Peter's face. He was sure he was quite red. His own lips pulsed, wishing to return the pressure. However, he stood still. There were promises to keep.

Emptiness washed through him as Havish led Flora out the door. His heart panged as she looked back. He turned away. He would not think of her round, sad eyes, her delicate feet walking out the door, her tear-stricken face. Instead, it was time to plan how to approach Caroline.

He waited till the next day to make his attempt. At Lapidary's jewelry shop he stood eying a pair of diamond earrings with a matching necklace. He winced at the price. It could be worth the risk. He pulled out his pocketbook, when a sick feeling filled him.

If he was going to marry Caroline, it would be on his merits alone. He would not flatter her with extravagant presents or false statements. He was an honest man. She had to accept him and the truth.

After buying a bouquet of flowers, he took the walk to the bakery. He opened the door, ready for whatever would be flung at him. However, Caroline was not there. Instead, her sister Nicole was behind the counter, bearing an amused, menacing smile.

"Caroline claims to be ill," she said. "Heartbroken, in fact. I've taken over for her until she recovers. I think she's just waiting for you to crawl back. She's at the house. I am sure Mother is prepared with some dramatic scene. If you would please go, my sister can return, and I don't have to spend so much time in the shop."

Peter made the walk down a few blocks to the Durbin's home. He raised his hand to knock on the door, when Mrs. Durbin threw it open.

"Good day, Mr. Talbot," Mrs. Durbin said. Her glare bore through him, seeking to melt him into slag. "How may I help you?"

"I... I..." He swallowed. "May I speak with Caroline, please?"

"If you've come to mend with her, yes," Mrs. Durbin said. "If you've come to break her heart further, then you may go."

"I wish to mend things, ma'am. May I speak with her?"

Caroline's voice came from the sitting room. "I will see him, Mother."

Peter removed his hat. It was the same bowler hat he had worn when attempting to face Adeline Winkleston. Hopefully, this interview would end better.

Caroline sat in an armchair, dressed in a plain skirt and blouse. A pile of wet handkerchiefs were beside her along with a half-eaten box of chocolates. Peter stood before her, bending the brim of his hat.

Handing the flowers to her, Peter said, "Caroline, you're a good woman, and I... I'd be sad to lose you. I..." He swallowed. "However, I don't think I have anything to apologize for. I've not had any affairs, and been honest with you." He shifted his feet as he looked down. His shoes needed a good polish. "But, to... to prove myself, I had Mr. Havish find new employment for Miss Flora, and I have… I have let her go."

His throat closed. He had let Flora go. He was a fool. How could he be so cruel to the young woman? However, he had made his choice.

"I have given our engagement much thought, Mr. Talbot," Caroline said, her words practiced and crisp. "I thank you for coming, but I think it is best if we end things."

His hat fell from his hands. "I fired Flora for you."

"It comes too late." She looked up at him, her eyes pale from tears. "Your sisters came to visit me yesterday, and told me how you threw them out of the shop. I did not believe it at first. I know your sisters exaggerate. However, Miss Crimson came by and confirmed the story.

"Papa has often told me that the way a man treats his sisters shows how he will treat his wife. I'll not be shouted at. I do not believe you were unfaithful with Miss Primrose, but I worry that you defended her so strongly. If I am to marry a man, I am to be the most important woman in his life. I think that is reasonable for a wife or fiancée to expect."

She held out the box containing her ring. "Goodbye, Mr. Talbot."

Peter blinked, wondering if he were in some extended nightmare.

"William and Charlie had just quit," he said. "I was overwhelmed…"

"There is no excuse for treating a woman like that."

He ran a hand through his hair. His eyes scanned the room for an answer, for something to change Caroline's mind.

"Why don't you…" Swallowing, he steadied his feet. It was better to accept what was. "I don't want the ring back. It is yours, and, well… it'd be a bit awkward for me to keep it. You can sell it, if you want. You could go on and use the money for your dowry." He picked up his hat. "I hope you find a more suitable husband, Miss Durbin. You're a good woman."

He walked past Mrs. Durbin, her face pale, her eyes wide, her lips searching for words that did not come. Peter nodded and muttered a goodbye before exiting the Durbin's house for the final time. As he strolled away, Mrs. Durbin's shouts rattled the windows, her demands of how Caroline could turn down a decent man echoing down the street.

Peter had shown himself a fool. Steadying his bowler hat, he grunted at himself. He should have known marriage was not for him. He was better off focusing on his shop and making shoes. It might be a lonely existence some nights, but it was one he understood.

Act III

The True Bride

Chapter 8

The first evening of Peter Talbot's return to bachelorhood was celebrated by his two brothers-in-law kidnapping him from the shop after closing. They took him to the bar and got themselves slovenly drunk. They toasted his independence and his triumphant tossing out of his sisters. They pined over bachelorhood, leaning against each other as they discussed youthful exploits that burned Peter's ears. They laughed heartily, patting Peter on the back, and congratulating his narrow escape of the jail of marriage.

He helped his two brothers-in-law home, neither sober enough to walk straight. Returning to his shop, he reaffirmed to himself that women and marriage were not worth the trouble. He understood too little of either subject.

Not even taking the time to change, he dropped onto his bed and stared at the ceiling. The night would pass more easily if he could talk to Flora. However, he had sent her off. He could try to bring her back, but, though his engagement was gone, it'd appear suspicious to do so. And, would she forgive him? He could not bear going to speak with her, only to have her glare at him with deserved anger. It would be better to let her go and start a new life.

The days somehow carried on. His sisters were in protest and refused to come clean. He hired a cleaning lady. She muttered madly to herself as she dusted and mopped, but did not shout at him. It was an improvement. He bought his dinners at the bar and often sat alone. There were conversations now and then with other men, but they always ended quickly.

Though he hardly drank, he liked the noise of the bar. It was better than sitting alone with his thoughts.

Most nights, he lay in his bed thinking of how silly it was that a grown man slept in what was originally meant to be a closet. However, the other rooms smelled of Flora. He would enter the spare room, intending to clean up, but, instead, would sit by the work bench, staring at the unfinished shoes. He couldn't bear to touch them. If he left them as they were, perhaps Flora would come dancing through the door, his coldness forgiven.

Some nights, he sat in the master bedroom, staring at the bed. He wondered what Caroline would have thought of Flora's decorations, and how angry she would have been once she knew Flora had done it. He often dozed off and fell into a dream, only to start awake at a noise downstairs. He would run down to the workroom, expecting to see Flora huddling in the corner. She was never there.

For the first few weeks, Havish came in saying, "Miss Primrose seems well. She's finding a place at Gossamer's, and keeping up her studies."

After a while, Peter said, "Please, Havish. No more word of her. I need to let her live her own life."

One night, he sat staring out the window of the master bedroom, pondering what might happen if he went to see Flora. It would be better now that time had passed. If she agreed to come back, there'd be less rumors to worry about. The shop was a warmer place with her in it.

He lay back on the bed, and drifted to sleep. A dream washed over him and he saw Flora trapped in a glass jar, surrounded by flowers. It began to flood with water. She pounded against the walls, silently yelling for help. He lay on his bed, his body frozen and unable to move. She was soon submerged in the water, her hair spread out and floating around her like fine moss. Her eyes pleaded for his help.

Peter jerked awake, his cheeks wet from tears. Sitting up, he wiped his face and then stumbled to his bed in the closet.

However, sleep was far from him. He lay the whole night, wondering what to do.

In the morning, he left Caleb in charge of the shop and went out to make deliveries. He soon found himself outside of Gossamer's. The truck hummed as he looked at the window, but he moved on. He passed by two more times. On the final pass, he parked the truck down the street. He pressed his forehead to the driver's wheel. Stopping to say hello was just a polite thing to do. She probably had so many new friends, she would hardly have time to speak with him.

Taking a breath for courage, he stepped onto the street. He rubbed the stubble on his chin, wishing he had taken the time to shave during the last week. He entered the shop, scanning for any sign of Flora. A few pretty young women chatted together as they lay gloves out on a table. Another girl was showing a pair of gloves to a gentleman who seemed more interested in the girl. However, there was no Flora.

Mr. Gossamer, a tall man with dark hair and a well-manicured mustache, leaned over one of his worker's shoulders. He glanced up and approached Peter.

"Good morning sir. How may I help you?"

"Hello. I'm Peter Talbot, the shoemaker."

"Ah. Yes. Many of my customers seem fans of your work. What can I do for you?"

Peter tried to keep his shoulders straight, but they kept hunching. "About a month ago, Mr. Havish sent you a former employee of mine named Flora Primrose. I was wondering if I might see how her new job is going."

Mr. Gossamer raised an eyebrow as he frowned. "Miss Primrose left her position nearly a week ago, Mr. Talbot. I am getting weary of men coming and asking for her. If you will excuse me, I have a business to run."

Peter's heart battered against his ribs. "Do you know where she went?"

"What does it matter?" Mr. Gossamer said. "I am glad she is gone. The girl was a nuisance. Always moping about, and putting on a show of dancing around. Men surrounded her, which drove my female customers away. I am sure you are glad she left your employ as well, and I thank you for sending her here to ruin my business."

"Thank you, sir," Peter muttered as he exited.

He started up the truck again, trying to keep focus on driving while wondering where Flora was now. He pulled up to the boarding house, not realizing he had driven there.

"She made her withdrawal notice last Tuesday," the matron running the house said. "She was quite worried. I told her to stay, but, she seemed too upset to listen. I hope you do find her. She is a lovely girl, and I would hate to see her in harm's way."

Peter felt a pang as he looked over the note, admiring how greatly her letters and spelling had improved. He thanked the matron, and headed to Havish's workshop.

"I've been checkin' on her 'bout once a week, sayin' hello," Havish said. "She's been mopin' about, but she didn't tell me anythin' of runnin' out of there. Don't know what to say, Talbot."

"I shouldn't have sent her on her own," Peter said.

"At least we both see that now."

"We've got to find her. I've got to know she's all right... she's just a girl... an innocent..."

Havish folded his arms. "It's about time you called her a woman, and admitted to yourself why you want to find her."

"She's my responsibility," Peter said. "I pulled her out of the meadow... She helped my shop... It's my fault she's gone."

"Why does she matter to you?" A smirk formed on Havish's face. "She's just a girl."

Peter shook his head. "Everywhere I go in the shop, I feel her missing pres
ence. When I try to sleep, I have dreams... Last night's dream... It worries me. If I can just make sure she is safe, then I think I'll be able to sleep."

"You're sadder than a dog longin' for its master," Havish said. "I'll have my boys keep an eye out for her, and put the word out. I'll let you know if we find her. I just suggest offerin' her more permanent protection once you do."

Chapter 9

Peter began spending every Saturday and Sunday wandering parks and meadows. Sometimes he ventured into the forest. He would sit under a tree for a while, picturing Flora twirling and dancing through a clearing. She could not have disappeared so completely. There had to be some sign of her.

Sleep grew more challenging as each day passed, and he spent most nights making shoes. He would wake up with his face on the work table, polish on his nose.

After three weeks of this, he decided a change might help him rest. He made Caleb head manager of the original shop, and rented the rooms above to Caleb and his wife. Using his savings, Peter bought a storefront in North Town. At the end of the block, he bought a small apartment. It was more expensive than a house in the lower town, but meant a fresh start. However, he bought his furniture from shopkeepers in his old neighborhood. They needed the money more than the North Town shops.

He brought in three new shoemakers and a girl to take orders. He spent a week before opening training the workers how to properly make a shoe to mold to a customer's feet. This was what made him different than Cordwainer, and what would keep Peter in business. Once his new workers were ready, the shop opened quietly. Within a day, they were busier than the old shop, the North Town customers happy for the convenient location.

The weeks wore on, and Peter was glad to have the work. The quick pace of the day kept him from worrying about Flora Primrose. In the evening, he went on long walks. It cleared his mind, though he looked at each passing women, hoping one might be her.

Spring was coming to a close, and Peter was surprised to find Nathaniel Bronhart answering the ad for a bookkeeper. The man was almost two heads taller than Peter, with thick, sweeping hair, and a neatly trimmed beard. The reputation for dashingness and handsomeness was well earned.

Peter stuck to business at first, despite thinking of the primrose he had potted to take to Adeline Winkleston. What would have happened if Bronhart had not been there? Flora may have been better off if taken care of by Adeline.

Focusing on the intelligent and competent man before him, Peter said, "How was your wedding to Adeline Winkleston?"

Bronhart gave him a dark look. "You must not read *The Rosetown Journal.* It turns out her late father was a disinherited son of wealth, and she is the sole heir of his fortune. It appears I was no longer worthy enough, and the lady is now engaged to some man-about-town named Alvin Westengaard."

"The author?" Peter said. "Forgive me. I did not know."

Bronhart smiled. "From what I have heard, you know something of broken engagements."

Peter sat silently a moment, before returning the smile. "I suppose I do."

Bronhart began his work, and Peter found it impeccable. As Peter was invited to dinner parties with local shop owners, and then the lower sphere of the upper crust, Bronhart became an invaluable resource. The tall man coached Peter in social expectations and histories of important people. It made meeting the wealthy folk far easier.

In early summer, Peter received a personal invitation from Mrs. Hampnell, his first wealthy customer.

You are to be a special guest of honor at my annual Eight Wonders of the City Benefit Dinner for Orphans. This is a grand surprise every year, so be sure to tell no one.

I consider your fine shoes one of the newest, most fascinating things this city has to offer. It is a high honor, and I could not give it to a kinder, more generous man.

In honor of the night, I ask that you donate a pair of gorgeous footwear for me to wear. These will be auctioned off at the end of the night.

Glad to help the cause, Peter presented the shoes to Mrs. Hampnell. On the evening, he sat sweating in a curtained-off area beside the head table. Mrs. Hampnell stood impressively at the podium, barely visible through a crack between curtains. He stared at his shaking hands, wondering how a shoemaker could be shown off like someone important or interesting.

A curtain opened down the row, and applause filled the ballroom. Peter smoothed his thin hair and checked his collar. Three more curtains opened, and three more wonders were displayed.

"For nearly a generation," Mrs. Hampnell said, "Cordwainer shoes have been the best in the city. Though his shoes are beautiful, the man I am about to reveal has shown me that fashion can be both lovely and functional. Sometimes, I find myself wearing my heels to bed instead of slippers." Polite laughter fluttered from the audience. "I present you a miracle-worker of shoes, the owner of Talbot's Boots and Other Footwear, Mr. Peter Talbot."

The crowd applauded, the clapping echoing into a thunder. Peter focused on walking straight and trying to smile on his way to the head table. A servant guided him past four strangers, and to the chair beside Mrs. Hampnell's. At the round tables filling the room were many of his customers. Only one man was not smiling. Judging by the wildly swept hair and slicked goatee, this was Mr. Cordwainer himself.

Peter looked up at Mrs. Hampnell as she said, "Our next guest is an orphan herself. By some miracle, she was restored to title and wealth not two months ago. Her tale, as many of you already know, is filled with sorrow and hardship. I present Miss Adeline Winkleston."

The youthful beauty stepped from behind the curtain, smiling broadly as she batted her fan, waving a lace handkerchief as she walked. Peter rose politely as she sat beside him. He tried to smile, when she squeezed his arm and whispered, "It is good to have a friendly face here, Mr. Talbot."

She gave him a kind smile before focusing on batting her eyes at the crowd, taking in their applause. Peter stared at the familiar blonde beauty, wondering what Bronhart would feel if he were here.

"Now, a man who has taken this city by storm," Mrs. Hampnell said. "A man of mystery and letters, whose book of philosophy has challenged our greatest minds, whose most recent novel has captured our imagination and hearts, a man whose speeches and lectures ignite the soul and enliven the spirit. I present to you, Mr. Alvin Westengaard."

The curtain was drawn and author entered. Nathaniel Bronhart's good looks were just brass next to the golden handsomeness of Alvin Westengaard. As he smiled and bowed to the crowd, several ladies fainted. His blonde hair gleamed, his chin was square and perfect. He swung his fine cane as he swaggered to his seat beside Adeline. He kissed her hand and gave her a dashing smile. Peter adjusted his tie, trying not to feel so squat and invisible.

"Mr. Westengaard introduced me to our eighth wonder just a few weeks ago," Mrs. Hampnell said. "I was overwhelmed and impressed by her beauty and grace. Given Mr. Westengaard's marvelous way with words, I will let him finish the introduction. Mr. Westengaard."

The man kissed Adeline's hand again and walked to the podium. His deep, masculine voice echoed through the hall, his tones powerful and commanding. Peter felt he should admire the man, though his stomach twisted and churned.

"Good evening, ladies and gentlemen," Westengaard said. "I was shopping for gloves in Mr. Gossamer's boutique, when I came across something far more precious and delicate." Peter clamped his hands on his armrests, trying calm his heartbeat. "I immediately went to Madame Plesatti to inform her of the next great prima dancer. Though a mere girl, she bears such natural grace she could be a goddess of dance. And this speaks nothing of her beauty, which can puts the stars, moon, and even sun to shame.

"Tonight, we will be graced with the lady dancing to *Pavia's Dance of the Dying Lover*. Not only was it choreographed by Madame Plesatti herself, but it is the lady's debut performance. Next weekend, she will premiere at the Morveaux, taking the lead role in Sharia's *La Talentio*. And the following weekend, she will dance to honor my own wedding to the luminescent Adeline Winkleston."

The crowd burst into applause and cheers of congratulations. Adeline let out the barrage of giggles she had once directed at Bronhart. Peter stared at the stage across from them, both fearing and hoping he knew who was behind the curtains.

"Without further ado," Westengaard said. "Mrs. Hampnell's eighth and final wonder of the evening. A beauty beyond nature, a grace beyond anything the world has yet seen. I present to you, in benefit of this city's orphans, the debut performance of…" Peter pressed a hand to his chest, hoping it would keep his heart inside. "Miss Flora Primrose."

The stage curtain rose, revealing Flora crouched on the floor, holding her legs to her chest. Her auburn hair was loose around her, except where it was pinned behind one ear. On her feet were the blue shoes she had made. Peter forced air through his throat, though his lungs forgot how to operate. Then, he realized the stage was covered in a glass cage.

He leaned forward, hoping this was not his dream. Fortunately, there were no signs of water.

A violin began a tragic tune. Flora rose in her elegant fashion, her white dress light and floating around her, accentuating her movement. Sorrow creased her face, and her arms drooped like a wilting flower. The music rose in a single sweet line. She spun and pirouetted, leaping and moving with the melody. The rest of the orchestra joined, and her movements and steps became more wild and desperate. She leaped and bounded to the edges of the stage, as if she wished to break free, but then fell back elegantly from the barrier. It was a beautiful, heart-wrenching dance. The entire audience watched, enraptured and silent.

Peter knew she was not playing some part. She was trapped, desperate, crying for help, but unable to speak. He wiped a tear from his cheek, trying to hide the motion with a scratch.

Adeline leaned over and whispered, "She is marvelous, isn't she?"

Peter said nothing. He had failed Flora. He had meant to keep her safe, and now she was trapped and treated like a toy to be displayed for amusement. She was a sweet, living woman who deserved to be free. Yet, how could he help her? He was just a shoemaker.

The song ended on a single tragic note. Flora crumpled to the ground as if dying. The music ebbed away in a haunting close and the entire hall burst into applause. Peter pretended to clap as he joined the standing ovation. He kept his head down, trying not to glare at Westengaard's self-pleased grin.

Flora rose and curtsied. The crowd yelled for an encore. As the curtain dropped, an overdressed woman guided Flora off stage. Peter fell back into his chair. There had to be some way to excuse himself and go to her, tell her he was here. He could help her if he could just reach her.

When the room was quiet, Mrs. Hampnell said, "Unfortunately, Miss Primrose is very shy, and will not be joining us for the rest of the evening. However, our other guests will remain to answer all your questions."

The aristocracy crowded most around Westengaard and his future bride. When finished, or tired of waiting, they focused on the other honored guests. Only reluctantly did they remember

Peter. He braved a smile and gave yes or no answers, his eyes scanning for a sign of Flora.

The auction was held, and Mrs. Hampnell's shoes were sold at an extravagant price. Slowly, the evening wore to a close. Making his best attempt at propriety, he quietly thanked the now tipsy Mrs. Hampnell for the honor and took his leave.

On his way out, he passed by the stage and ran his hand along the glass. He moved behind the platform, seeking a sign of Flora. It was almost as if she had only be a dream. Two tall, broad men stood with folded arms, forming a wall in front of a curtain. Peter moved to go past them, when one held out his arm.

"Can I help you?"

"I just wanted a word with Miss Primrose."

"No one sees her without Westengaard's permission. Good night, sir."

Walking away, Peter's hands tightened into fists. Whatever was happening with Flora, he would find her and free her.

Chapter 10

He woke just before dawn, a plan forming. Entering the shop early, he grabbed the stack of orders and flipped through the pages. He let papers fly from his hand and strew across the floor as he searched.

"Mr. Talbot? Is everything all right?" said the rose-cheeked Miss Beston as she came in to do her duties as cashier.

He peeked at the young woman before turning back to his search. "Fine. Fine. Everything is fine."

Crouching beside him, she began picking up the tossed about papers. "Can I help you find something?"

"No... I..." He stared down at the crumpled sheets in his hand. "Do we have an order from Madame Plesatti?"

"Yes. One came through last Thursday." She flattened the pile in her hand. "It was sent to the other shop yesterday."

Peter dropped the stack of orders, letting them scatter. "Thank you."

He ran out the door and to where the truck usually sat. It was gone, already out on delivery. If only his employees were less efficient.

With no other transportation, he sprinted down the street. At the end of several blocks, he leaned on a pole and huffed. A motorcar cab was just beginning its daily run, and Peter hailed it.

"Talbot's Boots on Dabbler Street," he said as he leaned back in the seat.

Each second of the drive dragged on far too long. Once the cab arrived outside his old shop, he handed over the fare and said, "Wait for me."

Peter shoved open the door and pushed past a pair of customers. As he reached the cashier's table, he grabbed the stack of orders and began sifting through them. He was close to his one chance to see Flora. It had to be here.

"Hey! You can't go there!" said a young man, marked as an employee by his cobbler's apron.

Caleb rose from sizing a client and said, "Harvey, that's Mr. Talbot." He jogged over. "Mr. Talbot, can we help you?"

"Madame Plesatti. I need her order. It's urgent," Peter said.

"Plesatti?" Caleb scratched his chest before jabbing his thumb toward the workroom. "Jim just finished half of it. It's a delicate piece of work. What do you want with it?"

"Make it your top priority," Peter said. "Bring it to me directly when it's done."

"Of course," Caleb said. "Everything going well, sir?"

"Yes." Peter set down the papers, this time making sure to straighten and flatten them. He flexed his cheek muscles before giving a weak smile. "You're doing good work here, Caleb. Fine work."

Peter rubbed his chin and walked toward the door. He paused as he caught a glimpse of his half-buttoned, untucked in shirt. His coat was tangled in itself, his chin covered in stubble. He raked his fingers through his uncombed hair and marched out to the street. Hopefully, this wouldn't send more rumors around.

That became doubtful as he discovered Molly waiting outside the door. Her fists pressed against her hips, her chin was raised, and a glare as sharp as jagged glass bore down on him.

"Ah, Mr. Fancy has come to walk among the peasants," she said. "The high life getting to be too much for you?"

"Good morning, Molly." He kept moving toward the waiting motorcar. "I am glad to see you well. How are your children?"

Hefting her hips to block his path, she said, "I imagine you've been too busy to know that Miss Durbin's engaged to William Harper. I am glad he sees the value of a good woman."

Peter paused his step and raised his head. A vision of Caroline and William began to form, but William's stooping shoulders seemed mismatched with Caroline's rounded curves.

"Give my congratulations," he said. "William's a good man. I hope his business is doing well… And, give my regards to Mary and her children." Peter took a breath. Molly might be angry, but she was still his sister. "If you'd like, you, Mary and your families are welcome to join me for dinner this Saturday."

"Too high-minded to come here for dinner?"

Opening the door of the waiting cab, he said, "If you want to come, just send word to my store uptown."

He escaped into the motorcar, leaving Molly glaring in the street. Settling back on the bench, he let out a breath once Molly was no longer in the cab's side-mirror.

"To Havish's shop," he said.

As the motorcar parked, Peter leapt out the door and ran to Havish's office. It was empty.

"Can I help you, Mr. Talbot?" said Dan, Havish's eldest son. The man was nearly as broad-chested as his father.

"Your father. I've got to speak to him."

"Dad's out on deliveries. Is all well? You have trouble with the latest load we sent you?"

"No. Your work's as fine as ever." Peter pulled out his handkerchief and wiped his sweating forehead. Though the office was partitioned off from where they soaked the skins in lye, the fumes were still strong. "I'll leave him a note."

Dan leaned against the doorway, his thumbs tucked into his belt loops. "What're you and Dad up to, Mr. Talbot? Mom's worried about the look Dad gets after he talks to you. It's the look he gets when he's havin' fun stickin' his neck out for other people. Usually ends up with him discoverin' another cousin or two."

Peter attempted a smile, but his muscles froze partway through. "Nothing at all, Mr. Havish. Nothing at all. Just some… gardening we're trying to do."

"Gardenin'?" Dan scratched his beard, just as his father did. "Eh. Right. I'll leave you to make your note."

Peter went through the torrent of papers on Havish's desk till he discovered a blank one. On it, he wrote: *I've found the flower, but it's in a cage.*

Leaving the note on Havish's seat, a warm calmness spread through his chest. As he rode in the cab back to North Town, an excitement amplified through him, coming out through his fingers tapping out a rhythm on his knees while he whistled softly.

His plan might not work, but there was at last some hope. He would get Flora free, and not let her go again. A proposal would be the best option. He grinned at the thought of holding her close, not worrying what anyone else might think, knowing she'd be with him for all his days.

At the end of the day, Peter sent his workers home early and closed the shop up himself. As he finished the final sweep, he lingered. There had to be a way to finish the shoes sooner. He leaned on the broom as he thought, when a knock pounded on the window. Peter jolted upright and ran to door. He opened the door, and there stood Havish with a broad grin.

As Havish entered, he said, "What's all this about a flower, Talbot? You found her?"

"Yes," Peter said as he locked the door behind the tanner. "But she's in trouble."

Peter smiled and rubbed his hands together as he told Havish of the gala the night before, and Madame Plesatti's guards blocking him from Flora.

Havish leaned his elbows on the counter, a deep frown on his face. "Mighty strange goings-on. How're we goin' to reach her?"

"Madame Plesatti's got an order with the shop," Peter said. "I'll deliver it, and see what I can do. Past that, I'll need your help."

"You know I'll do what I can for the poor girl." Havish winked. "She's my cousin, after all."

On Thursday, Madame Plesatti's completed shoes arrived. Peter put them in the delivery box and hurried to her studio. The windows were open, releasing the sound of a piano thumping out a tune and a woman barking directions for the dance. A banging soon joined in rhythm, echoing from the hollow floor. The woman's voice became shriller, when the piano and banging came to an abrupt halt.

As the woman shouted, "You there," "Your feet aren't bricks. Lift them up," and "Like a swan, not a canary," Peter approached the two broad-shouldered men blocking the door. Even with his hat on, they were at least a head taller. Several other men loitered nearby, shuffling their feet before passing longing glances at the door.

"Sirs," Peter said, his lips stretched into a down-turned smile. "I have a delivery for Madame Plesatti."

One guard held out his hand. "I'll deliver it."

"I'm Peter Talbot, of Talbot's Boots. They're delicately made. I want to make sure they fit right before I head back to the shop. I wouldn't want Madame Plesatti's feet to be uncomfortable. That's a... that's a dancer's livelihood, you know."

Peter let out a breath as one of the men stepped inside. After a muffled conversation on the other side of the door, he returned and said, "Follow me."

Peter's heart pattered within his chest as he was walked through a hallway draped with purple velvet curtains. The passage opened up to an office, dark green velvet draped across the walls highlighted with sprigs and ribbons of gold. The chairs were stiff and high-backed.

The shouting from the dance floor ended, and a few moments later a woman of middle-age glided through the doorway. Her body was lean, as if all of her dancing had stretched out her limbs. Peter forced himself not to shrink back as she gave him a glare capable of freezing him solid.

"You are Mr. Talbot, I presume." She slid into one of the chairs, crossing her ankles in one smooth motion.

"Yes, Madame." He gave a quick bow and held out the box. "Just… just delivering your shoes."

Raising one of her legs and giving a balletic point of her toe, she said, "Well, check them, if that's what you're here for. I hope they are worthy of your reputation."

"They are, Madame. We make sure all our shoes are up to standards."

Peter removed the shoe and tried not to gag. Her toes were gnarled, thick calluses and dark-colored spots along the foot. The arch was mangled from years of leaping and twirling and flying across the stage. It was a wonder she could still walk, let alone dance.

As he placed the new shoe on her foot, he said, "Funny thing, about the gala the other night. Your new dancer, Miss Primrose, she used to work in my shop in lower town. I've been worried about her, and I'm glad to see her taken in by a fine lady like yourself."

"And you hope to see her?" Madame Plesatti said.

"If I could… I know she's busy, with all the dancing she's doing, but…" He attempted another smile, but was sure this one was squeamish. "Might be nice for her to see a familiar face."

"She seems to prefer being alone," Madame Plesatti said.

Peter barely kept his shoulders from drooping as he finished buckling her shoes. Standing, he said, "There we are. Why don't you take a quick walk around the room and test them out?"

Both of Madame Plesatti's painted eyebrows rose, but she glided to her feet. She took a tentative step, when her eyes widened, and her mouth opened. With a few more steps, her gait smoothed and she spun in a tight twirl.

"They need to be broken in a bit to be really comfortable," he said.

Once she stopped, she said, "If I had only known." She lifted her leg high, her foot rising level with her shoulders. "They are beautiful. It is like walking on a cloud."

Peter swallowed. It might be his only chance. "If you like them well, can I ask a favor?"

She lowered her leg and raised her eyebrows.

"Can I have just a moment to say hello to Miss Primrose? Just to wish her well in her new career. She looked a bit... sad in her performance."

"She was performing a tragic romance," Madame Plesatti said.

"Yes. Right... but... even a girl of her talent needs a bit of encouragement from an old friend."

She looked down at her shoes, turning her feet to admire them. "Westengaard is very protective of my new protégé."

"The blue shoes she wore for the performance... I made those... well, she helped."

Madame Plesatti looked at him. "They are beautiful shoes, and so perfect for her." Her lips pushed out into a pout. "Well, he may not be pleased, but I think he won't mind a mere shoemaker."

She led Peter through another hallway and to a small room. His legs attempted to buckle as he stood in the doorway. Flora sat curled up on a chair, her head to the side as she stared dimly at nothing.

"Miss Primrose," Madame Plesatti said. "Do not tell Westengaard, but I have brought a friend to see you."

Madame Plesatti motioned for him to step forward. Flora turned her head languidly, when her eyes widened and her whole body snapped upright. She shook her head, the fear in her eyes warning him to stay back.

He wished they were alone and he could just put his arms around her. He would tell her he and Havish had a plan, that she'd soon be safe. However, Madame Plesatti was a few feet away, waiting.

"I just thought I'd stop in to wish you well, Miss Flora," He swallowed and attempted a smile. "I know I've got a few things to apologize for. If you need anything, you know, shoes or... anything." He raised his eyebrows, hoping to pass off as much information as she did with a glance. "Send word, and I'll do what I can for you."

She nodded her thank you before looking to Madame Plesatti.

"I'd better go. Don't want you to get in trouble with Mr. Westengaard," Peter said. He was about to step out, when Flora raised her arms, trying to mimic something. She waved her hand as if making a spell.

"Sometimes I think she is half-mad," Madame Plesatti sighed. "But, she is the best dancer I have ever seen."

Flora grabbed a flower barrette from the dressing table and waved her hand as if putting a spell on it. Peter shook his head, trying to understand, but knowing time was short. Her shoulders slumped, the pleading in her eyes returning.

He scratched his head and said, "It'd be easier if you had your voice."

She nodded emphatically, making the magic wand motion again before grabbing her throat.

"You'd best be going," Madame Plesatti said. "She seems upset today."

Flora gripped the chair, her eyes following Peter as Madame Plesatti ushered him out. He looked at her as long as he could, but, too soon, the door closed and they were separated again.

Chapter 11

During the next weekend, the Morveaux Theater was surrounded by men, all pressed together hoping to get inside. Peter was grateful for the ticket Madame Plesatti had sent him along with orders for more shoes. Several men were snarling and punching as Peter wove his way to the theater door. He let out his pent-up breath as he arrived at his seat and waited for the show to begin.

Flora floated across the stage, her body folding and flying in another tragic dance. Peter wished he could run and pull her off the stage, just take her to safety. He wished he could send her a note, however, it might be found by Madame Plesatti or Westengaard. Instead, he was left to sit still, watching her dance through her sorrow.

During intermission, he glanced at the boxes above. Westengaard sat alongside Adeline, chatting and laughing. The man was tall, his body firm and strong. Why had the man practically locked Flora away? It made little sense. There had to be more, but Peter could not be sure of it.

That night, he lay in bed, thinking on the matter, sleep a distant hope. After a while, he paced his apartment, and then dropped into his arm chair and stared at the wall. His chin lowered to his chest as he drifted off, when a scratching sounded at the door.

Wondering if he shouldn't have taken a first floor apartment, he approached the doorway. Looking through the keyhole, he saw a wet dog's nose sniffing at him. Peter checked the lock. It was sturdy and secure.

The dog scratched and let out a whine. Peter held onto the doorknob before opening the door a little. A large hound sat there, its shaggy fur matted with mud, one of Flora's blue shoes in its mouth. Peter opened the door further, when the dog dropped the shoe, barked, and scampered off into the night.

Using a handkerchief, Peter picked up the shoe. He sat down in the armchair and stared at it until the morning came. Mechanically, he went through the motions of getting dressed for the day. With the shoe tucked away in a sack, he carried it up the street to his shop.

"Good morning, Mr. Talbot," said Miss Beston as Peter entered. He waved his arm and grunted in return before entering his personal office.

With the shoe laying on the table, he turned it over and looked more closely at it. Teeth marks marred the delicate work of the fine shoe. How had the dog found it, and why had it been dropped on Peter's doorstep?

His breath cut off as he discovered a folded up paper tucked in the shoe's toe. With his hands trembling, he unfolded the paper. There lay Flora's writing, better than it had been, but still a bit crooked. Rubbing his chest to quiet his heart, he read the few words on the paper:

> *Peter,*
>
> *I have little time. I am always watched. Too many dangers here. Song on other side will explain.*
>
> *Flora*
>
> *P.S. My true name is Nerrelanthia. Or just Nia. I like Flora better.*

He turned the paper over. Above a set of notes and lyrics was written:

Sing and understand.

Open the window and fly with the wind,
Walk by my side and be my shadow,
Listen to my heart and uncover my mind,
I am hidden, lost far, far below.
I am hidden, lost far, far below.

He stared at the notes. How would this music help him understand anything? It mostly reminded him how long it had been since his mother had forced him to learn piano. He could still plunk out notes, but it gave him a headache. His brow furrowed as he tried to hum the tune. A piano might help him now.

He huffed out the last note, and the paper shimmered, a glow flowing across it. With a shout, Peter dropped it, the shimmer disappearing. Peter pushed his chair away from the table and stared at the letter.

He knew Flora had magic. She had shown him a few things, yet glowing paper was not something he was used to. He rubbed his forehead as he leaned back. The letter lay on the table like a foreign lump.

Flora was in trouble. He needed to do something to help her, and whatever that shimmering would do might be key. For Flora's sake, he had to try.

His shaking hands lifted the paper once more. His nasal tenor bounced across the melody. He hoped it was close enough. He sang the last word, when the center of the page began to brown and smolder. A small flame spread out. Peter dropped the letter on the floor and stamped on it. The burning circle grew, and white mist billowed out, filling Peter's vision. He ran forward and reached for the door handle, but his hands passed through nothing. He stuck his arms out, but there was no wall, no chair, no table, nothing to grab onto. Soon, the floor beneath him was gone, and he was just floating weightless in some sort of cloud.

He kicked his feet through the air, and tried to move his arms as if he were swimming. It did not help. He dropped his arms and shut his eyes. If he closed them long enough, he might wake to discover he had only hit his head.

His stomach lurched as he dropped several feet and landed on solid ground. The haze cleared around him. He blinked, and found himself in the muddy street of some outpost of a town. His feet hovered over the ground, yet felt as if standing on glass. He looked up as a prison wagon girded in solid iron passed, draft horses trudging forward. A face pressed against the one window, the crosshatched bars shadowing the man. Peter frowned as recognition muddled through his brain. The square jaw masked by dirt, the blue eyes glaring out, the thick waves of blonde hair marked this as Alvin Westengaard.

Peter turned to keep watch on the window, wondering how both he and Westengaard had arrived here, when a group of guards on horseback rode by. Their wide-brimmed, bowed hats were pulled low over their foreheads, with neckerchiefs tied around their collar in the manner of riders from the Surris Mountains. Peter had seen such men in a few rodeos down at the fairgrounds, but never this close.

In the midst of the riders was a man wearing torn and tattered Sandarian robes, a worn turban wrapped around his head. Peter let out a breath as he recognized the man.

"Rompell!" Peter shouted as he ran alongside Adeline Winkleston's foster father.

Rompell's face looked younger than Peter remembered. There was a hardness to his jaw, a deep hate in his eyes as he kept focus on the prison wagon. He did not seem the sensible businessman Peter knew, but a warrior from some adventure story.

Peter called his name again and reached out to touch Rompell's leg. His hand went through the leg and horse as if they were not there. Peter jumped back with a shout. He spun on his heel, looking at the crowd around him. He stopped as he saw Flora standing with another girl who looked enough like her to be her sister, though not quite as pretty.

"Flora!" he said as he ran over to her. He went to touch her shoulder, but his hand passed through, a tingling needling his fingers. He rubbed them together. They felt real and whole. He patted his chest and clothes. Everything seemed good and solid as usual.

"Where are we?" he said. "What's happening?"

Flora looked past him, her eyes wide as they followed Westengaard in the prison wagon. White mist billowed in, the creak of the wagon and clop of horse hooves fading along with Flora herself.

Drums pounded out a joyful rhythm as guitars played out a jig. Peter slapped his hand to his leg, wondering how he could be so aware in a dream. The air began to clear, and silhouettes of young women circled around him. Their skirts spread out as they twirled and leaped, their grace as great as Flora's. Giggling and laughter mixed with the musical instruments.

The air cleared just as a dancer passed through him. It was like a zap of electricity from head to toe. Peter hurried toward one of the gigantic trees surrounding the clearing. It would take three men to encircle each trunk, its reddish bark cracked and thick. Far above him rose the fir branches, the sun distant but warm.

To a young man laughing and playing the jaunty tune, Peter called, "Excuse me, but... I'm not sure where I am."

The man ignored him and ran his fingers across the guitar strings.

"Hello?" Peter's voice became a shout while he tried to keep his tone polite. "I'm not sure how I got here. Could you help me?"

No one responded. He rubbed his hand on his vest. He felt real. He could smell the pines, the earthy dirt, could feel the light, cool breeze and warm sun.

All worries over his own realness stilled as he spotted Flora dancing among a group of girls. They were all graceful, their arms and legs arching beautifully, but, somehow, Flora's steps were lighter. She hooked arms with another girl. They laughed as they spun together.

A rifle fired in the distance, the boom cracking in the air. Peter ducked. He did not want to test if bullets would go through him.

The musicians stopped and everyone went still like deer listening for a hunter. Peter walked to Flora and said, "What's going on?"

Her blue eyes scanned the forest. Another gunshot came, this time mixed with the sound of dogs barking. A man on horseback galloped into the clearing, his broad saddle laden with ropes and full saddlebags. He looked like the riders from before. Peter glanced at the trees. They matched pictures of the Surris Mountains. He couldn't be here, though. It took at least a week's train ride from Pippington, followed by riding on horseback up steep dirt paths with a guide. Few wagons made it back this far. He couldn't have just floated here from his shop, and Flora should be in Madame Plesatti's dance studio.

The rider stopped beside Flora and the girl who appeared to be her sister. The crowd gathered around him, the laughter gone.

"Delvin, what's going on?"

Peter stared. The sweet, gentle voice was Flora's.

"A prisoner escaped from the Culparr Mines." Delvin looked out at the whole crowd. "He's as dangerous as any one of those warlocks. Get in your houses and board the windows. Don't look strangers in the eye. The Rangers are out hunting him."

"How did he escape?" Flora said.

"Doesn't matter, Sis," he said as he turned his horse to leave the clearing. "Get yourself and Zarra to safety."

He kicked his heels into the horse's haunches, and it burst into a gallop. The dancers and musicians scattered in pairs into the forest. Even without moving, Peter found himself gliding alongside Flora. A dizziness filled him as trees blurred past, but he stood still. Zarra kept close to Flora, their hair loose as they leaped through the forest, jumping over ferns, around bushes, their feet light and quick.

A predator's roar echoed around them, reverberating through the forest. Flora and her companion went still and crouched near a tree.

A dark green dragon dove through the canopy, a rider saddled on its back. Its tail snapped as it let out another cry.

Peter jumped back. He had seen dragons ridden in the races, but nothing so large and close. There was a vast difference between a racing dragon and the behemoth speeding past him.

"Nia, we need to keep going," the similar girl said.

"Yes, Zarra," Flora said as her gaze followed the dragon.

They ran a ways further. The dogs grew louder, and another dragon passed overhead. Flora and Zarra reached a thicket of ferns and brushed aside a layer of pine needles and leaves, revealing a thick, warped, wooden door. Together, they grunted and opened it before running down the stairs and into a dirt tunnel. Peter ducked his head as he followed them into the cramped space. Zarra grabbed a lantern hanging on the wall and sang a few notes to it. A warm light glowed. Flora sang a brief tune and the door creaked shut.

"Which prisoner do you think it is?" Flora said as they went deeper into the tunnel. Peter walked beside her. It was less disconcerting than just floating along.

"Does it matter?" Zarra said. "If one can get out, then the others can too."

"The Rangers will find him…"

Her voice trailed off as a rumbling ran along the ceiling, horses pounding the earth above them. Both young women hunched down as clods of dirt dropped from the ceiling. Zarra gripped Flora's arm as if steadying herself. Once the hooves were gone, they squeezed each other's hands and gave each other a heartening nod.

The tunnel narrowed, and Flora took the lead as Zarra kept the lantern high. A noise clicked behind them and Zarra turned. "What's that?"

Flora stopped to look, when dirt and rocks crashed in, dust rising like a powder. Peter reached to grab Flora, but his hands went through her. The rocks settled as darkness enveloped them, broken only by a glimmer of light shining through gaps in the pile of rubble.

"Zarra?" The yellow light highlighted the soft curves of Flora's face and eyelashes as she prodded the pile of dirt.

"I'm fine. And you?"

"I'm safe." Flora said before humming a tune and pushing her hand toward the dirt. A spray of grit flew back, but the rocks did not budge.

"Be careful!" Zarra pushed the lantern through a hole. "The rest of the ceiling's likely to follow if anything moves. I'll go back up and use the path across Bucker's hill. The warlock won't be fool enough to travel on an open road. I'll meet you at home."

"He is more powerful than a common sorcerer," Flora said as she took the lantern from Zarra. "He could be centuries old, and cunning. Be safe."

Peter looked into the darkness, wondering where Flora was leading him and what she wanted him to see.

The air cooled as Peter followed Flora deeper into the tunnel, the dirt soft and ash-like beneath their feet. Flora's breath echoed in the narrow space as the darkness pressed against Peter's shoulders. The pounding of hooves rumbled above, shaking the roof and sending pebbles clattering against the side. Flora pressed on, holding her lantern high and watching the darkness ahead.

"Flora? You can hear me, can't you?" Peter said as he kept close to her.

She paused, turning her head as if she heard something. Peter stepped toward her. "Flora, what is going…"

She began to walk forward, when a dirt-laden hand reached out from the darkness and grabbed her. The lantern swung in her hand, scattering its beam of light as she cried out. Peter lunged to grab Flora as she cried out, but his hands passed through air. The hidden captor gripped Flora's shoulders, forcing her still. She shook as the man grabbed the lantern from her and raised it.

Hunching in the tight space, his blonde curls stiff with mud and in need of a good trim, his face laced with webs of grime, was Westengaard.

Letting go of her shoulder, he pressed a finger to his cracked and red lips and whispered, "Help me. I am innocent."

Her eyes wide, her breath short, she ripped herself. Before she could dart away, Westengaard hooked his arm around her waist and pulled her tight against him.

His voice soft and soothing, he said, "Rompell, the Sandarian who brought me, he is the sorcerer. The murderer they seek. The Rangers don't believe me. They will kill me if they find me. You must hide me."

Flora shouted as she kicked and writhed, when Westengaard clamped his hand over her mouth. "Don't lead them here."

"Now sir, you've got to let her go," Peter said, his voice like a dull thud, no echo coming from it.

Peter stepped closer, when Flora bit Westengaard's hand and his hold loosened. She sprinted a few steps away, when Westengaard lunged forward with a growl. He grabbed her arm and yanked her back, her hair tossing like a willow's leaves in the storm. Gripping her collar, Westengaard dragged her head toward his and forced a kiss on her. Flora cringed and shoved against his chest. Her arms loosened, though, and her body relaxed. Running her hand along his arm, she leaned into him.

"Hey! That's not... you don't..." He grunted as he tried to grab a rock. Any projectile would do, as long as his hands stopped going through them.

Westengaard released Flora, and she leaned back, smiling with the sweetness of young love. The blank adoration in Flora's eyes sent Peter scrounging for a larger rock.

"Where is the best place to hide, my love?" Westengaard stroked Flora's cheek.

"My family's farm has a cellar where we keep supplies for winter," she said. "It's not far."

Westengaard kissed her hand. "Thank you, darling."

Peter cringed as his fingers went through another rock. Then, he was pulled forward as Flora and Westengaard strolled through the tunnel, their hands together. She skipped along, so light and innocent, tricked into forgetting the danger beside her.

Peter rubbed his head as he followed. He seemed to be fully awake. However, the tunnel, Westengaard, and Flora herself had to be her memory. This wasn't possible, but it was the best answer he had. If she had brought him here, what did she mean to show him?

He looked again at Flora's eyes watching Westengaard with such sickening adoration. His stomach clenched. Adeline Winkleston had worn a similar look the other night at Mrs. Hampnell's gala. If Westengaard had done the same spell on both women, it would explain why Adeline had dropped Nathaniel Bronhart like a bag of rubbish. It did not, however, help Peter understand how to break Flora free from whatever prison Westengaard had her in now.

Westengaard and Flora stopped as they reached another doorway.

"If I go to the surface, they will find me," Westengaard said. "Do you know any transformation spells?"

Flora shook her head. "I only have common household magic."

Westengaard rubbed his fingers together as he scanned the wood entryway. "I have a little magic myself, but it is weak from being in the Culparr Mines." He held out his palm to her. "I will show you how to transform me into a dog, and I will follow you around until it is safe for me to escape."

"My brother is an Apprentice Ranger," she said as she set her hand in his. "Our dogs are trained to notice strangers, especially those using magic."

"It will be your magic, so they won't sense mine."

Flora pressed her lips together. "The dogs don't follow me around... but... the swans, geese, and ducks do."

Westengaard kissed her hand. "Then, shut your eyes and picture a handsome swan."

Flora closed her eyes. "I'll try."

Westengaard hummed a melody, and Flora sang it without words. Air swirled around him as he shrank down, his hair and clothes spinning out and turning into green, brown, and gray feathers. As the air and dust settled, a duck sat where Westengaard had been.

Picking him up, Flora said, "I'm sorry, my love. I tried... but... Ducks may be less beautiful than swans, but they are far kinder."

She sang to the door and a blue light ran across the edge before it swung open. With Westengaard in duck-form tucked under her arm, she went up the steps carved into the earth. Peter followed her through a small patch of woods, and then to a common farm yard. Ducks, geese and swans swarmed around her feet as she crossed the grounds. The air was filled with a cacophony of honking, quacking, and clicking.

"Now, lads and ladies, quiet down now," she said, giving them a false-stern glare. "No need to be so excited."

She opened the cellar and ushered the birds inside. As the last one entered, a sweating, red-faced Zarra ran into the yard.

"Nia!' Zarra said as she reached the cellar. "What are you doing?"

"Protecting my birds," Flora said.

"There's a warlock loose. He's not going to bother your geese."

Flora rubbed her finger along the transformed Westengaard's beak. "I'd rather have them safe."

Zarra shook her head before joining Flora in the cellar and helping shut and bar the door.

A queasiness bit at Peter as the events around him sped forward. Flora and Zarra climbed up a narrow set of stairs and entered the main room. Their mother and father hugged them.

As Zarra and Flora hunkered around the table with the rest of the family, everything faded. Peter floated for a moment, before finding himself standing in a small bedroom. Flora lay on the bottom bunk, Zarra on the top. Flora watched the moon rise as she held the duck form of Westengaard close to her chest. Peter stared into the beady eyes of the creature. Westengaard seemed much less formidable as water fowl.

As Zarra let out a light snore, Flora climbed out of her bed and pulled a worn gingham dress over her nightgown. Peter looked down, hoping to hide the blush on his cheeks. Even if she couldn't see him, he could still be a gentleman.

Westengaard waddled after Flora as she crept across the cold, wood floors of the narrow, cramped farmhouse. It was a series of rooms which may have once been a set of chicken coops. The floor creaked. Flora paused her step. A few light snores echoed, but there was no other sound.

She went outside and across the yard to the barn. As she tacked the horse, she cooed and rubbed its side. It nickered at her, but remained still as she worked. Once she was done, she pulled two full knapsacks from beneath a hay stack and hooked them on the saddle. She mounted and Westengaard fluttered up to sit behind her. With a click of Flora's tongue, the horse set off at a quick walk, the group of fowls trailing after her. They quacked and honked in excitement until she whistled a tune, and they quieted.

Once clear of the yard, she kicked the horse into a trot. If floating alongside someone was dizzying, floating alongside a trotting horse was nauseating. Peter hoped the beast wouldn't gallop.

Upon reaching a small lake nestled in a valley, and Flora slowed her horse to a stop. She dropped onto the forest floor and listened to the wind passing through the trees. Peter scanned the sky. It was beautiful and clear, and something he would like to share with Flora if they were both really here, and she weren't helping a fugitive escape.

A popping sound mixed with a hum, and Westengaard unfolded into human form again. Flora ran to him and he caught her hand and kissed it. "Thank you. I will forever remember your kindness."

She blushed, and turned her tear-filled eyes away. Westengaard placed his foot in the stirrup and pulled himself up. As he swung his leg around, the horse reared. Westengaard's foot slipped, and he thumped to the ground. As the horse galloped off into the forest, Flora ran to Westengaard's side.

Dropping to her knees beside him, she said, "Are you all right?"

Westengaard pushed her arms away as he stood. With a crick of his neck, he said, "Why didn't you stop the horse?"

"I was worried you—"

He grabbed her by the collar. "I'd be fine if I had a horse to get out of this cursed wilderness."

She shrunk back, her eyes wide. He snorted as he let go, and then paced the clearing. Kicking at rocks, he muttered to himself.

"The Caldons live nearby," she said. "We can get another horse from there."

Westengaard stopped his pacing and looked at her. Taking her hand, he spoke in a deeper, softer voice. "I am sorry for my temper, my love. It is only my death I fear."

He kissed her cheek and Peter glowered.

Waving his hand, Westengaard said, "Lead the way, my love."

Flora clung to his hand and smiled dreamily as they stepped through the forest. Peter stomped behind them, wishing he was really there and could walk between them, breaking apart their clasped hands.

"There must be a way to prove your innocence," she said. "Misonwood is a beautiful place, isn't it? We could be happy here, together, if you stayed."

"I have argued my innocence many times," Westengaard said as he pushed aside some low branches. "And even given them the names of witnesses. I can no longer sit in a prison for Rompell's crimes. I must be free and live on."

"Where will you go?"

"Wherever magic is forgotten and unused, and I can live out my days in peace."

They went on in silence, their feet cracking across pine needles and dirt. After a while, Flora said, "My brother and father say there is little magic in the rest of Barthan, and especially in Pippington. We could start a happy life there."

"Do your brother and father often go there?"

"Only once every few years for the rodeo. I've never been. Delvin says it's dirty and cramped, but I've seen pictures. It looks wonderful."

Westengaard touched her arm and motioned for her to be silent. Peter followed their gazes up, when loud flapping approached. Keeping hold of Westengaard's arm, Flora led the way into a thicket near a fallen tree trunk. As they crouched, a deep blue griffin dipped down through the canopy, the moonlight reflecting off its massive feathers. Peter dropped to the ground and curled up, its claws coming toward him. An elk leaped out of the bushes, and the griffin claws dug in and carried its dinner away.

Peter forced himself to uncurl and breathe. He groaned as he began gliding alongside Flora again. She and Westengaard ran toward another tree, seeking better coverage. They paused for breath, until the barking of dogs approached. A horn sounded, followed by the roar of a dragon.

"Is there a cave or tunnel nearby?" Westengaard said.

"Delvin said they started searching them yesterday. None will be safe."

Westengaard held her hand between both of his as he said, "You have already helped me get this far. I will take my chances alone. Go home and be safe."

However, he made no move to run. A smirk twitched at the edge of his mouth as Flora looked up at him with adoring eyes.

"Without you, I have nothing here," she said. "I know these forests, and can get you to the train station down the mountain. Let me help."

Peter grimaced as Westengaard kissed her.

"Thank you, you brave, darling girl," Westengaard said. "I will hum the song again, and add my magic to yours. Just picture something fleet of foot, that can run quickly."

She nodded, and they sang the tune again. This time, Peter noticed a thread of white light forming around them. It swirled, a popping and humming following. Where Westengaard and Flora had been, now stood a buck elk with a magnificent rack of antlers, and a slim female elk. They stayed close before leaping into the forest. Peter shut his eyes as he was dragged with them, hoping it would ease the dizziness. It didn't.

Chapter 12

Time sped along as Peter was zipped through the mountain range. Three dragons with riders closed in on the supposed pair of elks dodging and swerving through the forest. Peter ducked as one dragon dove down, its claws outstretched and ready to grab Westengaard. The false-elk swerved around one of the massive trees, and the rider yanked on the chain bridle, pulling the dragon's head up, barely stopping the reptile from slamming into a tree.

Another dragon circled ahead of them, where the mountainside became a cliff. Behind them, the other two dragons formed a perimeter. Westengaard ran straight for the cliff and leapt, Flora in doe form following after. Somehow, their feet remained steady as they went down the sheer slope. Peter shut his eyes for as long as he dared, trying not to picture himself crashing onto the ground. It seemed harm wouldn't come here in Flora's memory, but he'd rather know he'd soon wake safe and whole in his shop.

Peter groaned as his body tilted to follow the two false-elk as they reached level ground. They ran along a narrow path through thick brush, and to the bank of a broad river. Westengaard stepped into the shallow water by the shore, when a pop echoed and he returned to human form. A few seconds later, Flora was in her lovely form once more, though still on all fours. Peter glanced back as a warm, pink sunrise highlighted the mountains. Dragons came around a mountain peak and dove toward them like a hawk seeking its dinner.

"We need something that can swim," Westengaard said as he seized Flora's hand. They sang together, and then dropped as salmon into the river. The dragons swooped through empty air before rising into the morning sky and following the river.

Peter floated above the water for a few seconds, when he was pulled under. He could breathe easily, but still gasped for air. He ducked as he rushed toward rocks, swerving around them at the last second. The dragons flying above were warped by his view through the water, but he was sure they were getting larger by the moment.

He followed the salmon that were Flora and Westengaard down a narrow fork to the left. One of the dragons stayed with them, while the other two flew along the wider path, swooping over the river in search of the fugitive.

Westengaard and Flora swung through a set of rapids before swerving down another fork and into a deep stream. The dragon continued along the main river while Flora and Westengaard approached a calm pool under the shade of branches. There was some bubbling around them, when arms and legs seemed to flare out of the fish, and they were in human form again.

With a few kicks, Westengaard rose to the surface. Flora, however, tumbled and kicked, her dress and hair flaring around her as she scrambled to rise. Her hand reached out to Westengaard. He grimaced and shoved her shoulder, pushing her down before swimming to the shore. He pulled himself onto the muddy bank and panted for air. Rolling to his side, he coolly watched as Flora's dress caught in some reeds. She thrashed while her blue eyes were wide with fear, her cheeks bulging, holding in precious air.

Peter kicked his legs and swung his arms, until his feet hit something like solid ground. Pushing against the weight of the water, he waded to her side and reached for her arm. His hand passed through her as bubbles of air spilled out from her mouth, floating to the surface as she thrashed.

Flora had to make it. Peter needed the chance to meet her, and to have her help. She couldn't die here.

Her movement slowed as her eyes dimmed. Peter knelt down and dared reach for where her dress was snagged. He gasped as his hand met solid cotton. He tugged, and tore the fabric free. With a few kicks, she came to the surface.

As she swam to the bank, Peter marched on shore. If he could touch her dress, then he might be able to smash Westengaard's nose so it blended with his brawny chin. The man may be at least a head taller than Peter, and a warlock, but it was worth a try.

Peter huffed as he stood in front of Westengaard and pulled back his elbow. He let his fist spring forward. It went through Westengaard, sending Peter into a spin. As Peter steadied, the warlock ran to Flora's side. He gripped her hand, helping her crawl onto the bank. She coughed out water as Westengaard sat and pulled her into his arms.

"Oh, my love," he said, petting her hair and holding her close. Flora pressed her head to his chest and held his hand.

"You're a rotten man," Peter said.

The fugitive couple rose. Peter glowered and followed them deeper into the forest. At least time sped up again, turning the sickening sight of their clasped hands into a blur as they hiked. As the sun set, they found a small cave to hide in. During the moonless night, they scavenged for food, and then Flora slept, her head resting against Westengaard's shoulder.

Time wore on, and another day or two passed of hiking and hiding as dragons flew overhead, seeking them. As the forest became thinner on the second or third afternoon, the dragons no longer appeared. When Flora and Westengaard crossed into a valley lined with farmsteads and cottages, Peter understood why. Most people wouldn't want a dragon swooping in over their yard.

As a farmer stood alone in a field, pounding his pickaxe into the ground, Westengaard crouched through the tall stalks of wheat. Soon, he returned to Flora's side with the farmer's lunch pail and took the food.

"You stole from an honest man," Peter muttered, and then grunted. It was foolish to think honesty meant anything to a fellow like Westengaard.

Flora and Westengaard hurried on, though Flora's feet were lagging now and she limped a little. The edges of her dress were in tatters, just as when Peter had first met her. Once in an apple orchard, they hid under a tree, stealing apples, and eating the poor farmer's sandwich.

Westengaard sat up as a train whistle blew in the distance. Tossing away his unfinished apple, he said, "Come along, love. Not much further."

Half-dragging Flora and her tired legs, Westengaard led the way out of the orchard. He boosted her over a few fences as they cut across farms and lots lining the valley. The sun passed along its arch, the day turning to afternoon as they approached the train tracks. Westengaard's step quickened and Flora limped as fast as she could, but still falling behind. They finally stopped as a small train station came into view, the station no more than a platform and a ticket office.

As the station manager strolled along the wood slats, Westengaard and Flora went through the brush, crouching low until they were hidden just out of sight of the platform.

"We should find a place to rest," Flora said as she knelt beside Westengaard.

"We are getting a ride to this Pippington." Westengaard's sharp eyes focused on the distant track.

Peter sighed and tapped his hand on his leg as he watched them wait. Dusk settled in, and Flora let out a yawn. With her head on Westengaard's shoulder, she dozed off. If only it were Peter's shoulder instead, and she were safe. Everything would be much better once Peter helped her to real safety, away from this liar.

As the sky grayed into the edge of night, a group of six horsemen gathered on the opposite side of the tracks. Peter straightened, a dim hope rising. Then, he remembered this was the past. He looked back at Flora. She was not a flower yet.

Shaking Flora awake, Westengaard said, "We must run."

Westengaard's long legs drove across the soft earth, leaving Flora a few steps behind. The horsemen hepped and hollered as they galloped toward the fugitives. Flora tripped, her arms flailing as she fell. Peter reached for her arm, but his hand passed through.

"She's innocent," he shouted to the men. "It's only a trick."

The horsemen passed Flora and the invisible Peter, several men swinging lassoes over their heads. Westengaard sprinted, seeming to pick up speed. A rider tossed out a lasso with precision. Dropping in the dirt, Westengaard rolled across the ground. The lasso landed without catching its target. The horses closed in as he rose to his feet. He shook dust off his shirt and then raised his head before bellowing out a strange, low-toned song.

The horsemen shouted to each other and swerved just before several explosions spread up from the ground, sending out sprays of dirt. Horses reared and whinnied, shying away. Men struggled with the reins as the horses knocked into each other, several falling onto their sides.

One of the horsemen stopped to help the men pinned down by their horses, and the two who had gained control of their mounts moved toward the warlock.

Westengaard flexed his hands as he stepped back. He sang out a few notes and moved his arm in a sweeping motion. Both horses and riders were swept to the side. One of the downed men fired a gun. Westengaard flicked his wrist and a shimmering wall formed in front of him. The bullet cracked through and clipped his shoulder.

With a shout of rage, Westengaard punched forward. Flame erupted around his arm, swirling like a mess of snakes. A line of flame pushed out from his feet. The fire touched a dry bush, and flames began to spread out across the empty land.

Flora ran past the edge of the fire and to Westengaard's side. The two riders climbed on their horses and whistled while circling their arms. Gusts of wind encircled the spreading flame, containing it. One of the riders dropped his arm, and galloped toward Westengaard. As he approached the line of fire, his horse shied to the side. He dropped to the side of his saddle and then let go, sending himself tumbling across the ground.

"Delvin!" Flora cried as the man rose.

Her brother rose, his pistol steady as he approached Westengaard.

"Hand over my sister," Delvin said, his face covered with grime and sweat.

Flora leaned against Westengaard. "He is innocent. You must believe him. Tell them the truth, please, love."

Delvin's scowl deepened. "What did you do to her?"

Westengaard grabbed Flora and pulled her in front of him. Keeping an arm around her waist, he said in mocking tone, "We are in love, boy." He brushed his hand on Flora's cheek. "Can't you see her loving dedication?"

The wheeze of a train's breaks echoed from the station as Delvin charged forward. Westengaard threw Flora out of the way and then rammed his elbow into Delvin's chin. Delvin flew back, losing hold of his pistol. Westengaard grabbed the gun as it tumbled through the air, and then aimed at Delvin.

"Please. He's my brother. Let's just go," Flora said, tugging on Westengaard's arm. "He will let us be if he knows you will keep me happy and safe."

The train's wheels clacked across the tracks, still moving slowly as it came closer.

Holding his arms up, Delvin said, "You've won a few hours. Keep her safe until we come to rip your hide."

"A gentleman's offer, indeed," Westengaard said just before he pulled the trigger.

Delvin shouted and grabbed his thigh as the bullet hit. As he fell into the dirt, Flora began to run to him. Westengaard gripped her arm, jerking her back.

"He'll be fine," he said. "I'm sure there's a healer among them."

She pulled against his grip while reaching out for her brother's hand. Westengaard grabbed her around the waist and dragged her toward the tracks. She kicked and shouted, fighting against the warlock's grip.

Peter stared at the wound in Delvin's leg before chasing after Flora. Perhaps he could do something again.

Once near the tracks, Westengaard twisted Flora around to face him and forced his kiss on her. She jerked, but then calmed, her eyes softening with adoration.

With an empty smile, Westengaard said, "Everything will be all right, my darling."

The train began to pass, slowly picking up speed. Westengaard pulled Flora over his shoulder and ran beside it. He grabbed onto a ladder and pulled them onto the train. With a few sung words, Westengaard ticked his head to the side, and the door of the car slid open. He tossed Flora in before jumping in himself. Peter cringed as he was launched through the air and into the car with them.

Time sped by once more, Flora on the floor among crates and boxes, curled against Westengaard's side, Westengaard holding a hand to the wound on his shoulder. Peter paced the cramped space, glancing out the door, hoping to see Pippington soon. He needed to get back to the present. He needed to reach Flora.

The train's brakes screeched, announcing their approach to a station. Westengaard leaped out of the train, and caught Flora after she jumped. They tumbled down a grass hill while Peter was lurched alongside them. Once on their feet, the fugitives ran into a familiar aspen forest.

The gray of dawn highlighted the trees around them as Flora and Westengaard entered a meadow of daffodils. Peter rubbed his thumb on his vest as he looked out through a gap of trees. There was Pippington, though entire neighborhoods were missing, and the Grandor building was still under construction. That had been completed almost a decade ago.

He dropped his hand as a chill pricked along his back. Turning around, he knew Flora would soon be rewarded for her forced devotion.

"They will be looking for both of us," Westengaard said. "I have enough of my magic left to help you hide while I find somewhere safe."

Flora smiled and squeezed his hand. "I will wait."

Westengaard returned her smile and lifted her hand. He led her into a gentle spin while singing a soft tune. As she turned, she shrank until becoming a pink-blossomed primrose sitting in a field of yellow daffodils.

With a smirk, Westengaard brushed his palms off. "Stay safe, love."

As Westengaard strode toward Pippington, Peter knelt beside the flower and said, "Everything's going to be all right, Flora. I've seen enough."

However, he remained in the meadow, the seasons moving swiftly around them. Snow came and went, but the blossom remained. The years turned, the city expanded, countless people strolled through the meadow. He sat close to the primrose, wondering how lonely she must have felt sitting here alone, forsaken by Westengaard.

Chapter 13

Time returned to normal speed and Peter looked up as his former-self appear in what had once been his best suit and bowler hat. Peter winced and shut his eyes. Though it was the day he had brought Flora to his shop, he'd rather not follow himself to Adeline Winkleston's doorstep, and watch his failure again.

As he peeked through his fingers the mist returned, folding around him. It ebbed away as he now stood in Gossamer's shop. A herd of men surrounded the counter, grinning as Flora pressed against the wall beside the register, her eyes wide and face pale. Where she had seemed lighter than air in the forest, here she seemed pinned down by her dark green dress and bustle. Men snatched gloves from the shelves without really looking at them and pushed toward Flora.

The shop bell rang, announcing the entrance of Westengaard in a fine suit and vest, Adeline Winkleston on his arm. As she laughed and chatted with the man, her eyes carried the same blind adoration Flora had borne through the entire escape.

"Mr. Westengaard," Gossamer said, pushing through the crowd of men. "You'll have to pardon the excitement. Got the new line of gloves in, but I've saved a sample for you."

"Thank you," Westengaard said. "My darling fiancée was hoping to wear them for the wedding."

Flora dropped a box of gloves, the little color in her face evaporating. Several men bent to grab the box, when their heads knocked together. A shout broke out, and then the pound of a fist to flesh. Other men began to climb into the brawl, when, Gossamer yelled, "Enough!"

He pushed the men apart and fought his way to Flora.

"Miss Primrose. My office. Now."

Peter wished he could press a hand to Flora's shoulder as he followed her to Gossamer's office. Her eyes remained down, but she held her chin up as she stood in front of Gossamer's desk.

"I understand now why Mr. Talbot foisted you on me," her employer said. "How can a man run a shop with all your flirting? It is unprofessional to have all of your fellows visit during the day. I have tried to be charitable, but I can no longer do so. Miss Primrose, I must let you go."

He pulled an envelope from a drawer and held it out to her. "There's your day's wages. I hope you'll be wiser with future employment."

Tears dropped down Flora's cheeks as she stood holding the bills in her hand.

"Get along, Miss Primrose. No good waiting for something to change. I have three daughters and know better than to succumb to such crying."

She took a faltering breath and wiped her cheeks with a handkerchief. Her head down, she stepped out of the room and onto the shop floor. Westengaard stood by the office door, leaning as he faced Adeline and continued their bright conversation. Flora raised her shoulders and pressed toward the door, her steps faltering as she glanced at the crowd of men watching her through the window. Peter paced the floor. He was a miserable fool for letting her go from his shop and come to this point.

"Westengaard, look at the poor girl," Adeline said as she tugged on his arm. "Perhaps we can help."

Flora's knuckles were white as she clutched her handbag and quickened her step. Westengaard used his long stride to pass Flora and block her path. Flora tried to skirt around him, when Adeline stood in her way.

"Miss Primrose, was it?" Westengaard said, his voice smooth, and warm.

Flora's whole body trembled as she looked up into his smiling face, his eyes bearing a lack of recognition.

Hooking her arm through Flora's, Adeline said, "We heard Mr. Gossamer. No girl should be treated so." She looked to Westengaard. "We can give her a little help. Don't you think so, dear?"

Flora pulled her arm away and shook her head.

"What do you say, Miss Primrose?" Adeline said, patting Flora's shoulder with a fan. "Come now. We all fall on hard times. Isn't our duty to help when we can?"

Flora pointed at her throat and tilted her eyes toward Westengaard.

Adeline laughed. "Oh, you poor dear. I should have known. Most women are tongue tied around my dear Westengaard. Let's step outside, and we'll be able to find somewhere to chat in private."

"Miss Winkleston, she can't speak," said one of the shop girls. "She has no voice."

Adeline pouted and squeezed Flora's hand. "How dare Mr. Gossamer! What a cruel man. Come with me. We'll find you better employment, and if I cannot, I am sure my papa can."

Flora held onto Adeline's arm to keep herself steady as Westengaard walked on her other side. Westengaard opened the shop door, and stood in the way of the crowd of men. Adeline put a king arm around Flora's delicate shoulders and led her to a fine motorcar with fringe along the window. As the chauffeur held open the door, Flora hesitated.

Adeline rubbed Flora's shoulder and said, "Go ahead. There is nothing to fear."

Flora turned her pleading eyes to Adeline, yet then climbed inside. Peter followed her in and found a narrow spot on the bench beside her. This would be better than floating alongside the vehicle.

Once Adeline was seated Flora, Westengaard shut the door and said, "I shall meet you at the mansion.

Adeline leaned her head out the window, and Westengaard kissed her cheek. The chauffeur turned the crank, and the motorcar puttered alive. As they jostled along the street, Peter stared at Flora's hand, so close to his. He wished to have the warmth of her fingers against his, his grip reassuring her, telling her everything was going to be fine. Yet, as he glanced out at Westengaard's tall, stately form, Peter wasn't sure it would be.

The motorcar drove down a few streets and avenues as Adeline prattled on about Westengaard's wonderfulness. Peter felt as sick as Flora looked. At last, they passed through a set of rod iron gates, cherub statues on either side, and drove up a gravel driveway lined by tall, carefully manicured hedges. The path ended at a fine porch with marble pillars, stained glass embedded in the double doors.

"I could not ask for a better man to marry," Adeline said while leading Flora up the porch and into the recently inherited mansion.

Peter whistled as he stared at the gilded window frame. It was far finer than the simple house Adeline had grown up in.

"Papa claims to approve of him," Adeline said. "But, sometimes, I'm not sure he does. They had some trouble in the past, but it is over now, and Westengaard has more than proved himself. One day, Papa will love him nearly as much as I do."

Peter stared down at the polished floor as he followed the women, no sound from his footsteps. As Adeline led Flora on a tour of the first few rooms, Peter put his hand in his pocket. It was empty, but there had been some of Rompell's smoke snaps earlier.

If Rompell helped imprison Westengaard, he might really be a sorcerer. Yet, Peter wasn't sure how to find out. It wasn't something he could ask Rompell outright. He rubbed his pocket as he hurried to rejoin the women before the spell whipped him over.

Walking into a sun room, Adeline went to a small desk. Setting out a notepad and fountain pen, she said, "Write your skills here, and we'll see what employment we can find."

Flora slowly sat at the desk and picked up the fountain pen. Her hands shook as she wrote: *Don't marry. Danger. Westengaard lying. He is a—*

The fountain pen shivered, and a splurt of ink splattered on the page, covering Flora's words.

Adeline frowned as she took the pen from Flora. Looking it over, she said, "They said it was the best quality. I'll have it returned tomorrow and get a less faulty replacement."

She pulled a pencil from the drawer and handed it to Flora. With a deep breath, Flora began to write again. She got through the word: *Don't*—, when the tip broke.

"It must be your shaking," Adeline said, patting Flora's hand. "Here I am, forcing you to think about your next position, when you have had such a difficult day. Let's walk in the garden while some tea is made."

They entered the garden, passing white rose bushes and bougainvillea vines. Flora looked around each corner as she arched her arms, trying to pantomime the truth about Westengaard.

With a laugh, Adeline said, "Yes, it is a terrible thing to just toss a kind girl out."

Flora jumped onto a bench and raised her arms, wiggling her fingers like a child pretending to cast magic.

Adeline laughed again before pulling on Flora's sleeves. "It has been a hard day. Sit down and enjoy the beauty of the garden."

Flora's shoulders drooped and she joined Adeline at an iron table in a courtyard. Adeline pointed around the courtyard and mentioned plans for the reception. Flora leaned her chin on her hands as she stared helplessly at Adeline. Peter stood across from Flora, wishing he could confirm what she was trying to say. Perhaps he could get a word with Adeline, if he ever returned to the present.

"Westengaard!" Adeline said as she leaped to her feet.

She ran to her fiancé and threw her arms around him. He laughed and kissed her cheek before gesturing with his arm. From around the corner appeared Madame Plesatti, as stern-faced as ever.

"Oh, Madame Plesatti," Adeline said as she nodded in greeting. "What an honor to have you here."

Passing the engaged couple, Madame Plesatti approached Flora. "This is the girl you spoke of?"

"Yes," Westengaard said as he took Adeline's arm. "As I told you in the street, our chance meeting was a matter of fate." He gestured toward Flora. "Miss Primrose is the essence of dance. You must let her audition."

Madame Plesatti circled Flora, her eyes narrow as she discerned the young woman's form. "I am looking for something fresh and alive, something pure, without all the show most dancers are putting on." She motioned toward the open courtyard. "Will you dance for us?"

Flora scrunched her shoulders and gripped the bench.

Adeline fluttered over and squeezed Flora's arm. "She has had such a difficult day. Let her audition in the morning."

"I prefer auditions to be raw," Madame Plesatti said. "It allows the dancer to move from the heart. Everything else can be taught."

"She will be magnificent." Westengaard held out his hand. "Come and dance, Miss Primrose."

Flora pulled her knees to her chest and shook her head.

"Leave her be. She is so nervous," Adeline said.

"Stage fright can be overcome," Madame Plesatti said.

Westengaard sat beside Flora and leaned close to whisper, "The Rangers are searching for us. We are both wanted for execution. Dance, and you will be able to hide among the ensemble."

Peter glared at Westengaard. "You rotten..."

He stopped as Flora stepped from the bench with her usual grace.

"Doesn't she need music?" Adeline said.

"A true dancer hears the rhythm of their heart," Madame Plesatti said.

Flora twirled in a sad circle before bounding across the courtyard, like an animal trapped and wounded. Each movement was smooth, sadness following the arc of her dance.

"Oh, Flora," Peter whispered. "I shouldn't have let you go."

She raised her arms up and collapsed into a curtsy.

Adeline clapped. "How beautiful. How delightful."

Westengaard joined the clapping with a polite smile. Madame Plesatti tapped her finger on her chin.

"She is not an ensemble dancer," she said. "Her grace would make the other girls look like dancing bricks. No. She must be the central jewel, and the others will orbit around her to help her shine.

"If you agree, Miss Primrose, I will have an apartment made for you at the studio, per Mr. Westengaard's arrangements. There, you will be protected from the prying eyes of men, and prepared for a debut Pippington will speak of for decades. Do you agree, Miss Primrose?"

Flora looked at Westengaard. He raised a warning eyebrow. With her head down, Flora nodded.

The mist gathered again as Adeline said, "Wonderful."

As the mist cleared, Peter stood in the dressing room at Madame Plesatti's studio. Flora was curled on a chair, her head hanging as she stared at the floor. Westengaard sat beside her, pressing close.

Taking her hand between his, he said, "Madame Plesatti is concerned you are not eating. I cannot tell her the truth—that you are ill for your love of me. For now, everyone must believe I love Miss Winkleston.

"However, I have come to give you hope, dearest Nerrelanthia. My wedding with Miss Winkleston is only a means to an end. Her father, Rompell, is the sorcerer who framed me and sent me to the Culparr Mines. He has built a life of lies here.

"I have found his secrets. The wedding is only a spectacle to gather the community, and make sure he can no longer hide from the truth. When it is over, they will know him for the foul man he is, and I will break him by breaking Miss Winkleston's heart."

He kissed her hand. "I need you to be well enough to help me. My victory will be worth nothing without you." He stood and squeezed her hand. "Be patient and trust in me, my love."

As he stepped away, a shudder ran along Flora's shoulders. Peter moved toward her, when the mist folded in around him again. He stepped forward, and found himself beside a narrow bed with a plain quilt on it. His cheeks turned pink as he realized Flora sat there in her nightgown, only the moonlight illuminating the room.

Flora leaned over a stack of papers, writing quickly, her brow furrowed with worry. Peter pressed his lips together as he squatted in front of her.

"Do you know I'm here?" he said.

She signed her name and held up the paper. Peter's mouth felt dry as he recognized the song which had led him into her memory. She folded it carefully and then raised her eyes, her lips thin and tight. Peter's heart jolted as their eyes met. A smile formed, softening her sadness.

"I'll find a way to help you," Peter said. "You just sit tight."

She rose to her feet with the light innocence she had carried in the forest, and placed the paper in her blue shoe. She glided to the window and opened it and she whistled. Dogs barked on the other side. She whistled a song to them, and then dropped the shoe. Peter floated out through the window as a dog caught the shoe and began running.

The air stung Peter's face as he flew alongside the hound through the streets of Pippington. Peter's surroundings became hazier as they approached the doorstep of his apartment.

"Peter!"

Peter turned his head, hoping this was Flora.

"Mr. Talbot!"

Something hard smacked his face followed by a splash of water. His surroundings blurred together, and then became black for a split-second. Someone struck his face again and shook his shoulders.

Peter gasped as his eyes opened. Above him was the ceiling of his office, and beside him was his desk. He lay on the floor blinking, taking in a deep breath to steady himself. Just as he began to sit up, Nathaniel Bronhart grabbed him by the shirt and shook him.

"Mr. Talbot… What happened?" Bronhart's face was lined with worry.

Peter prodded Bronhart's arm. It was firm, muscular, and quite real. "You can see me?"

Bronhart frowned as he released his hold of Peter. "What sort of a tumble did you take?"

Peter looked into Bronhart's eyes, the phantom of Adeline's blank-eyed adoration filling his mind. Gripping Bronhart's shoulder, he said, "The wedding's a sham. It's all a trick."

"What wedding? Are you all right?"

"Adeline Winkleston's wedding!" Peter held onto the table to help himself stand. His shirt was drenched in sweat and his stomach protested from a lack of food. "It's all a lie. You've got to help her."

Bronhart rose and smoothed his vest. "Sir, I have nothing to do with the woman. She has broken her relations with me, and I have no need to concern myself with her affairs."

"But you love her still, don't you?"

"Do you still love Miss Durbin?"

Peter scratched his head. "No, but…"

"Miss Winkleston broke her engagement. If it were a matter of life or death, I suppose I would help. Otherwise, I have no reason to connect myself with her again."

"It's a grave matter."

"Sit down, Mr. Talbot." Bronhart pulled out a chair. "You've got a fever."

Peter slapped his hand on the table. "She's in danger, Bronhart. Maybe if you just kiss her, it'll wake her up. Yes." He grabbed his jacket from the hook by the door. "That fixes anything, doesn't it? True love's kiss?"

Peter began to open the door, when Bronhart slammed it shut.

"I don't know how long you've been out, Mr. Talbot, but you're not well. You are fortunate I came to your office to say good night before leaving. No one has seen you all day, and the boys assumed you were out on business."

"I'm fine." Peter pulled on his jacket. "You've got to trust me, Bronhart. Just kiss Miss Winkleston and you'll see."

"I make it a habit not to woo women who have broken relations with me." Bronhart pressed his hand to Peter's shoulder. "If we are going anywhere, we are going to a doctor."

Peter shook his head. "There's no time. We've got to help Miss Winkleston and Flora."

Bronhart tightened his grip on Peter's shoulder. "A doctor, sir."

Peter let Bronhart push him out of the shop. Bronhart hailed a cab, and they rode to the clinic. Peter tapped his hands on the examination table and shook his leg as he endured reflex tests and thermometers. After an hour, the doctor said, "You seem a bit agitated, but in good health."

Once Peter was dressed again, Bronhart led him outside. "I'll walk you home."

Peter waved him off. "You've been a good help, Bronhart. Go on home. Just think I've been overworking lately. A long walk will do me good."

Bronhart eyed him. "Are you sure?"

"Yes. Go on home. You've been a great help."

Bronhart nodded before leaving. Peter smoothed his matted hair as he meandered in the opposite direction. There was too much to explain to Bronhart. If he didn't believe in magic yet, Peter didn't have time to convince him. Peter needed to talk to someone who would believe him, who could confirm what he had seen was true.

He began to walk toward South Town, hoping to find Havish at his regular bar. The tanner would know what to do.

Peter paused at a street corner as a truck drove by pulling a long trailer. Inside was a racing dragon. As it passed, the creature's tongue flicked out and it licked its arm lazily. It was far less ferocious than the mountain dragons in Flora's memory.

He looked up at the street sign to get his bearings. Hummingbird Street, only a block from Miss Winkleston's former home. Peter flexed his fingers. Rompell would have answers. Perhaps he already knew of the danger his daughter was in. He had to, if everything Peter had seen was true.

Yet, was he a sorcerer, as Westengaard claimed? All of Rompell's coin tricks and sleight of hand could be a cover for his real magic. If Peter wanted answers, he had to take a chance. Westengaard was not someone to face alone.

Peter drew in a breath, tugged his jacket straight, and ventured onward. Once on Rompell's porch, Peter tried not to remember his last visit nearly a year before. Setting his jaw, he rapped his knuckles on the door. He shifted on his feet and shoved his hands in his pockets while waiting.

How would he start the conversation with Rompell? He couldn't tell him a flower who turned out to be a girl said Rompell might be a sorcerer. How did anyone address a sorcerer? In the books they were usually villains, or seemed to start the conversation, already knowing what the person had come for. Well, if Rompell was a sorcerer, he may already have read Peter's mind, and Peter wouldn't have to introduce the topic.

The door opened to reveal Rompell in a plain, dark suit. With a puzzled smile, Rompell said, "Mr. Talbot. Good evening. How may I help you?"

Peter tried to smile as he said, "Well, I went out for a stroll and I was... I was just in the neighborhood, and... um... I thought I'd say hello and thanks for sticking with my shop, even with all the scandals and rumors blowing around."

Rompell's eyes narrowed. "You must have been walking a while." He stepped aside. "Why don't you come inside and have a drink?"

"That'd be great. Just great."

Peter followed Rompell into the sitting room where a light symphony played on the phonograph. The room was sparse, with only a painting of a garden resting on the mantle, a few pieces of furniture made of polished wood, and a pair of armchairs. Peter had always pictured the room adorned in rich Sandarian carpets, swaths of golden cloth, and pillows on the ground in place of furniture, just like the books described. This room seemed far too normal.

Rompell went to a cabinet and pulled out two glasses and a bottle filled with a pale gold liquid. As Rompell handed over a glass, Peter wondered if there were any charms or spells inside. He sniffed the liquid, and his senses were filled with a mix of cinnamon, nutmeg, citrus, and honey.

"Sandarian ale," Rompell said as he raised his glass in salute. "Have you had it before?"

Peter shook his head as he swirled the liquid.

"Always refreshing after a long ride in the desert," Rompell said. He took a sip and sighed. "I indulge in few things from my homeland, but this, has all the spices of home."

Peter took a sip. The alcohol burned a little, but the honey and citrus were refreshing and cool. Turning his glass, Peter said, "Do you think there's magic in it?"

Rompell gave his deep laugh. "Do not believe all rumors of Sandar." He held the glass flat on his palm. "Most things are exactly what they appear to be."

He waved his other hand past the glass, and the glass disappeared. Peter frowned, and Rompell laughed as he turned his hand and showed where he had hidden the glass on the table beside him.

Peter forced a laugh. "Clever. Very good."

143

He took another sip of his drink while flapping his jacket to cool himself.

"Let me take that," Rompell said.

Peter let the man take his coat. In the few seconds Rompell was gone to hang the jacket, Peter wiped his forehead with his already wet handkerchief. He looked around the room, seeking for a path into the conversation he needed to have.

As Rompell returned, Peter said as casually as he could, "How goes the wedding?"

"If you have read *The Rosetown Journal*, you know all I do."

"Letting your girl take full reins of the event?"

"My choices and opinions hold no sway over Adeline's decisions anymore."

Rolling the glass between his hands, Peter said, "I... er... I hope it's not prying too much, but it seems you don't approve of Mr. Westengaard."

A darkness shaded Rompell's face. "As I said, my opinions do not matter."

"Right... well..." Peter's voice raised in pitch. "I heard the strangest rumor the other day." He coughed and took a drink to clear his throat. After swallowing, he said, "My friend said Westengaard's actually a... He's a..." Peter took another drink for courage. The last words shot out. "A warlock."

He thunked his glass on the table, trying to hide the shaking of his hands. Rompell swirled his drink before taking a long, slow sip. All the warmth in his face was replaced by a cool calculation. "Where did you hear such a rumor?"

Peter dropped into an arm chair, his legs too faulty to remain standing on. His foot tapped as he rubbed his hands together. "Maybe I'm just mad, Mr. Rompell. This past year... You'll not believe me, unless.... unless what I've heard is true..."

Rompell sat across from him. "What have you heard?"

Peter dared look up. "That you're a sorcerer."

"I see. My secret has been revealed." Rompell rolled his fingers and a spout of flame appeared before fading away.

Peter jumped. "Then, it is true."

Rompell laughed as he rolled back his sleeve, revealing a lighter attached to a string on his thumb. Holding his palm flat, he flicked his thumb and held it there. A flame rose.

"I didn't know the street tricks I do for children was sorcery." He slapped Peter's shoulder. "I think all of your success is fraying your nerves."

"I'm doing all right."

"Financially, perhaps." Rompell swallowed the rest of his drink before standing. "Come on, Talbot. I'll drive you home."

Not knowing how else to ask about what Flora had shown him, Peter nodded. He pulled on his jacket, cranked the engine of Rompell's car, and then climbed in the passenger seat. As the engine puttered, Peter leaned his head on his hand and stared out the window. They were nearing his street, when he said, "You remember the flower I had in my old shop?"

"Ah, yes. A pretty thing."

Peter swallowed. "Turns out, it was a girl."

Rompell laughed. "Rest, Mr. Talbot, is the best remedy for madness."

"She's Miss Flora Primrose now. I'm sure you've seen her in the shop, and then dancing at the Morveaux. She sent me a... a letter this morning." Peter took a breath. If he was going to help Flora, he needed to be bold. "Said she saw you in Misonwood, out in the Surris Mountains about ten years ago, escorting Westengaard as a prisoner."

"She would have only been a girl. She probably confused another Sandarian for me."

"It wasn't a letter, actually... It was a little song she wrote, and all of a sudden I was there, alongside her memory. I know it sounds like madness, but..."

The tires screeched and Peter's head smacked against the dashboard. Rompell swerved the car to a stop. The engine still rumbled as Rompell turned and faced Peter. Peter shrunk back from the hardness in the man's eyes.

"These are things you cannot understand, Mr. Talbot. They are not to be trifled with, especially Alvin Westengaard." He spat out the name like it was a glob of dirt in his mouth. "I know the danger my daughter is in, and I have everything in place to protect her.

"Keep your distance, maintain your shop, and live your life. If things work as planned, Miss Primrose will be given her fair reward."

"She didn't mean to help him escape. She was under a spell… The same spell he's got Miss Winkleston under…"

Rompell slammed his hand on the seat. "I have said more than I should. Here in Pippington, magic must pretend not to exist. It is best you remember that. Keep to your shop and trust me."

Peter tried to hold Rompell's hard gaze, but then looked away. He winced before asking, "Just, if you could tell me… What is the difference between a warlock and sorcerer?"

"Age, Mr. Talbot. Sorcerers know they are mortal. Warlocks pretend they are not, and exist for centuries. If Westengaard were a warlock, you would be wise not to cross him."

"I see…" Peter dared look at Rompell once more. "If I can help, let me know."

Rompell let out a laugh before waving his hand at the door. "Good night, Mr. Talbot."

As Peter opened the door, he muttered, "Thank you, Mr. Rompell."

Once Peter's feet touched the sidewalk, Rompell's car screeched away. Peter watched the man go, wondering how many other secrets he kept hidden.

As Peter wandered back to his apartment, Peter knew he had to do something. Let Rompell worry about Adeline. Peter would make sure Flora got out of this safe, even if he wasn't sure he would make it himself.

The next morning, Peter hovered by the door of his shop before opening. At last, Havish came through the door, and Peter said, "I found out more about the flower."

Havish left the skins for one of Peter's workers to sort through and followed Peter to his office. Once the door was closed, Peter filled two glasses with light cider. As Havish leaned back in his chair and sipped his drink, Peter told him of seeing Flora and what he had seen in the letter.

When Peter finished, Havish said, "You're tellin' me you think Rompell's a sorcerer and Westengaard's a warlock?"

Peter pressed his hands together. "I know it sounds mad, but…"

"No more mad than a girl turnin' into a flower." Havish let out a grunt. "You sure what you saw is real?"

"It must be." Peter gripped the edge of the table. "Westengaard is marrying Miss Winkleston next Saturday. Flora's going to dance there, and we've got to help her."

Havish raised an eyebrow. "So, you're proposin' we break up a wedding?"

Peter took a breath. "I suppose so."

Havish grinned and raised his glass. "Then, let's do it for Miss Flora Primrose."

"For Flora," Peter said as he touched his glass to Havish's.

As the week trudged along, Peter listened as his customers and shop girl gossiped, hoping to hear anything about the wedding. Havish stopped by every evening, reporting what he'd learned from chatting with the tradespeople involved.

On Friday, Havish laughed in triumph as he brought in a map of Adeline's garden and the layout of the wedding tent. Peter poured drinks, and the two men huddled over the paper. Empty spools and broken pencils stood in as placeholders for key players as a plan took form.

Resting his elbows on the desk, Peter said, "I wish we knew what Rompell was planning."

"The man's clever," Havish said. "He'll find a way to work our plan into his. Let him take care of Miss Winkleston if he's not goin' to help us."

Peter stood up. "Perhaps he already has." He opened a drawer of his desk and pulled a canvas bag full of smoke snaps he'd been saving for his nephews. Hefting the bag in his hand, Peter said, "Rompell gave these to me. I think there might be magic in them."

Havish eyed the bag, a glint of a smile forming. "There's much trouble we could do with those."

Peter rubbed his neck as he looked down once more at the plans. "I hope so."

Chapter 14

The morning of Adeline Winkleston's wedding was marked by the sun rising, shining through the curtains and into Peter's face. He stretched out on his bed, the blankets twisted and tossed to the side after a restless night. Rolling into a sitting position, he tried not to picture Westengaard's tall form, nor what magic he had prepared. Whatever came today, Flora was all that mattered.

Repeating this under his breath, Peter strapped a hammer to his calf and slid his pinstripe pants over it. He pulled on the rest of his suit, buttoned his vest, and placed the bag of smoke snaps in his coat pocket. Pulling on his top hat, he looked himself in the mirror. Perhaps he should have tried to bring Bronhart into the conspiracy. At least that man looked as if he could fight a warlock.

Peter flexed his hands and pulled at his collar as he crossed through the streets. Soon, he joined the line of guests entering the white wedding tent set up on the grounds of Adeline's mansion. His stomach battered at his ribs as he passed Havish leaning casually against his truck. Havish winked before turning and pretending to polish the door handle. Peter was glad to have at least one friend here.

The line slowed, and the wealthy guests chatted at each other. Peter took off his hat and patted his forehead with a handkerchief, when a tall shadow blocked the sun. Gripping the hat to stop his hands from shaking, Peter raised his chin and faced Rompell. The bride's foster father wore a dark, fine suit, a red scarf hanging over his lapels despite the heat. The man's glare was far from friendly.

"A word, Mr. Talbot."

Peter's dry tongue stuck against the roof of his mouth as followed Rompell to a side tent.

"What are your plans?" Rompell whispered as he kept an eye on the passing guests and servants.

"Er… nothing much. Just to get Flora out… that's all."

Rompell pressed a hand to Peter's shoulder. "Find a way to get her out quietly, without Westengaard noticing." Pain flinched through his eyes. "I do not know if I can protect you if he attacks."

Peter's skin went cold even in the stuffy air of the tent. He attempted to smile, but it was more of a grimace.

"Have courage, shoemaker," Rompell said as he let go of Peter. "We will both need it today."

Rompell waved his hand, motioning for Peter to follow him. Leading the way past the waiting line of guests, Rompell pretended to laugh. "Very clever, Mr. Talbot. A man does have a spare sole if he has a good pair of shoes."

Once in the tent, Rompell disappeared through a side entrance, leaving Peter alone among the rows of white chairs filling the flower-drenched tent.

Nearby, Mrs. Hampnell and Petunia Ophombach leaned in close conversation, analyzing and critiquing each detail of decor. Other customers of Peter's gave him a smile and glimpse of their shoe as he made his way down the aisle. He tried not to hear the threads of gossip tangling through the room. A few older women touched Peter's arm, slowing him and inviting him to converse with their eligible daughters. He gave a polite nod, but quickly escaped using the excuses he had learned from Bronhart.

"Oh, I think I see a friend," he would say. He felt like a ball being swatted from conversation to conversation. Yet, in all of his searching and escaping, in all of the feather-ridden hats and petticoat-fluffed dresses, there was no sign of Flora.

Wiping the growing layer of sweat on his forehead, he approached the side entrance the wedding party would come through. Flora might be behind the curtain, part of a display before the ceremony. He was almost to the white, gauzy curtain, when a gruff man at least three times Peter's girth stepped through. His glare sent Peter scurrying back to the safety of the white chairs.

The chairs were filling quickly. He scouted for a strategic seat, near one edge or another. It might be better to wait there till Flora appeared as part of the spectacle, and then steal her away as everyone watched the ceremony.

His step paused as he saw Madame Plesatti. Seated beside her was a young woman, her face and hair covered in a pale pink veil. Peter pressed his hands against his jacket, hoping the pattering in his chest would quiet down.

It was her. It could be no one else.

Trying to keep his breath calm, he approached. Mercifully, Madame Plesatti's towering hat had left the seats behind them open.

"Is that you, Madame Plesatti?" He coughed, trying to cover the squeak in his voice.

She turned with an arched, stenciled eyebrow. A smile warmed the sternness of her face as she said, "Mr. Talbot! Did you get the orders I sent? I have hardly taken off my new shoes. Walking has never been so soft and light. Your shoes are a miracle of leather, and will bring a renaissance of dance."

"Er... thank you, ma'am." He fidgeted with his top hat.

"Are you going to sit there? I do hope you will. Miss Primrose is so nervous." Madame Plesatti lightly tapped Flora's shoulder. Flora kept her head down, her fists clamped to her skirt. "It will surely help to have a friend nearby."

Peter hesitated. Getting close to Flora wasn't supposed to be so simple. Taking the opportunity, though, he sat on the edge of the seat behind Flora. She turned and raised her head, staring at him through her veil. He kept his eyes on Madame Plesatti, his face warm under Flora's gaze. One full look at her, and he might lose his composure. If he kept his wits together, he could get her out.

"Now, tell me, Mr. Talbot," Madame Plesatti said, "How a man of simple means became such a fine and respected shoemaker."

Hoping it would pass time as the ceremony approached, he told Madame Plesatti about Havish giving him the blue leather, of Mrs. Hampnell coming to see the shoe, and then his expansion of business.

"Miss Flora's a good worker," he said. "One of the best shoemakers I've ever seen."

"She seems able to do anything," Madame Plesatti said as she patted Flora's arm and Peter attempted to smile. "But, I think she was born to dance. She has the grace of a nymph."

Madame Plesatti patted Flora's shoulder. Flora wilted in her chair, staring once more at the ground.

Turning back to Peter, Madame Plesatti said, "Miss Primrose also wrote that you were recently married. Where is your wife? Was she unable to come?"

Peter swallowed to wet his mouth before saying, "Well, I was engaged, but... uh... she decided I wasn't the right fellow for her."

Madame Plesatti shook her head. "How heartbreaking. How are you going to win her back, Mr. Talbot?"

"I... er... She's already engaged to another fellow..."

"How inconstant!" Madame Plesatti unfurled her fan.

Peter pulled at his ear. "Well, Miss Primrose, you remember William Harper? The old bachelor opened up his own shop, and now is engaged to Miss Durbin. I'm right happy for them. They're fine people and will have a good life."

"You are a kind gentleman," Madame Plesatti said, pressing her fingers to her chin as if he were a fascinating creature. "And brave, coming to another man's wedding."

He glanced at Flora, wondering if she could rescue him from this conversation. "Don't mind too much. Can't begrudge others their wedding day..." He met Flora's large, blue eyes. "I've come to see things set right."

Her eyes widened, when the sweeping hum of the string orchestra began, announcing the beginning of the ceremony, and the arrival of Westengaard.

Peter's hands bent the brim of his top hat. Women gasped and applauded at Westengaard's handsomeness as he stepped to the wedding altar. He smiled and squeezed the shoulder of the priest, giving a wink to guests in nearby chairs.

Peter rose with the crowd as the groomsmen escorted in the bridesmaids, all adorned in ruffles and finery. Flora held onto her chair to steady herself. Peter pressed his lips together before placing his hand on top of Flora's. A tingling ran up his arm as she turned her face toward him. He tried to give her a confident nod. Confusion pressed lines in her delicate face. He began to pull his hand away, when she wrapped her fingers around his and squeezed tightly. His entire body warmed and a smile broke through his nerves.

She let go as Adeline Winkleston entered alone. The young bride's dress was a mountain of lace, bedecked with jewels and beads, all glimmering and bouncing as she walked. Women sighed in admiration at the mess of bows and flowers. Peter's neck throbbed with his heartbeat as looked to the entryway, but there was no sign of Rompell.

Westengaard's smile was bright as he took Adeline's hand and led her up the steps to the altar. Peter flexed his jaw, trying not to scowl. The priest pushed back his glasses and opened his book to begin. The room went still, when a clear, sweet woman's voice sang out in a sad melody:

Hey nonny nonny hey, flowers and bows decorate the maid
Ho nonny nonny ho, but I warn you to be staid.
Hey nonny nonny hey, turn from the lady by your side,
Ho nonny nonny ho for I am the True Bride.

Heads turned, seeking the voice floating through the air. Peter stared at Flora, unsure if he had seen her lips move.

The priest looked back at his book, "Ah, yes. Friends, family…"

Flora sang again, this time walking down the row. Her eyes were distant as the soft lilt of her song rose in volume. Madame Plesatti stepped back, watching Flora without surprise. Peter held onto his chair. He wanted to follow Flora, but he could not make a scene. Perhaps there would be a chance to get her out quietly in just a moment.

Flora walked out of her row and into the aisle. She raised the veil and sang the song a third time. Adeline's face paled, her eyes wide and fearful as she faced the distraction.

Attempting a smile, she touched a hand to her head, rubbing her temple. "My love, what is this?"

Westengaard stood still, dramatic shock across his chiseled face. With his arms arched and eyes wide as if hypnotized, he walked down the stairs toward Flora and her song.

Adeline grabbed Westengaard's elbow. "My love, is everything all right?"

He ripped his arm away and spun around to face her. "Witch!"

"What?" Adeline said, cowering under his furious gaze.

"Oh, you play your innocence well." Westengaard tossed back his head, before facing the crowd. He threw his arms wide. "Now it is all clear, Adeline. Your deceit. Your betrayal. Your cruelty."

Adeline stepped back, holding her bouquet to her chest as if it could protect her. "Westengaard, I don't understand…"

"You filled me with a poison that passed through my veins and burned the fire of desire in my breast." He pounded his hand against his chest as he stood over her, righteous indignation electrifying him. "I saw the signs, but the spell made me too blind. Your wealth is false, a lie you enchanted men into believing. Your father was no heir. He was a common soldier, no greater than any other. Oh, to use your spells to gain wealth, and then to steal my heart. But, its rightful owner is here, Miss Adeline. Your reign is over, and I am at last free."

Adeline bobbed as if about to faint, and one of the bridesmaids ran forward. With a moan of pain, Adeline dropped her bouquet and held her hands to her head.

"It is finished, Adeline," Westengaard spat as if she were a dog worthy of kicking.

Adeline's legs failed, and her bridesmaid caught her shoulders. The bride's jaw clenched and her face became as white as her dress as Westengaard strode toward Flora.

Peter looked over his shoulder, but Rompell was nowhere to be found.

"My heart knew my true bride when she first danced," Westengaard said. "She had such sorrow for the prison I could not see. I was bewitched and blinded by this woman…" He glared back at Adeline. "This witch who has lived among you, feigning purity and innocence. But, I tell you, her core is rotten, corrupted with dark magic."

Holding his arms out to Flora, he said, "But now, I am free of the curse, and we are at last reunited."

Gasps and whispers rippled through the crowd. Peter pushed past the gaping audience on his row. It was too late to hide.

His top hat fell off as stumbled into the aisle and ran to Flora. Grabbing her shoulders, he stopped her advance. She pushed steadily against him, her eyes glazed and distant.

"Flora, you can't do this," he said. Awareness broke in her eyes. She looked at him with pleading and despair. Still, she pressed forward and sang again.

"He's the one who cursed you, remember?" Peter said. "He's the fellow who left you behind and betrayed you. Don't go to him. I… I…" He swallowed before whispering, "I love you, Flora."

She stopped. With a sob, she threw her arms around Peter. Their lips met and lingered together. Warmth pulsed through him as he held her tightly, unwilling to let this sweet moment go. The crowd and their thousands of eyes, the orchestra, Adeline's massive dress, the warlock glaring at them, all ceased to exist. All that mattered was this woman, kissing him in a way that was quite improper in public. And, he liked it very much.

"Peter," she whispered, her voice soft and sweet. "You broke the spell."

He grinned before kissing her again. They clung to each other, when a disdainful laugh echoed through the tent. Keeping his arms around Flora, Peter looked up at Westengaard. The warlock glared at him like some pest about to be crushed. It was a good time to leave.

"You think you can steal my true bride?" Westengaard's voice echoed through the tent.

Peter stood in front of Flora as Westengaard advanced. Peter's heart pressed against his ribs, seeking its own escape. Taking a breath, he reminded himself of the hammer and smoke snaps. Even if Rompell wasn't here, he had a chance.

Trying to stand a little taller, Peter said, "If you'll excuse us, we should be going."

He put his arm around Flora's shoulder and she leaned against him, her whole body trembling. They turned toward the main exit and began to walk away from the failed ceremony.

Westengaard, however, strode past them and blocked their path. His lips curled into a tight, cruel smile as he whispered, "Of all the men who have come to save their proclaimed loves from me, you, sir, are pathetic."

Giving Flora a sweet, longing look, Westengaard held his hand out to her. Most women would melt before that look. Flora pressed tighter against Peter.

"Come, Nerrelanthia," Westengaard said, his voice booming through the room. "Step away from this common fool. The spell is broken, and I am ready."

"She told me the truth. You're a fugitive," Peter shouted. Gasps rang out. He hoped someone would go for the police. Hopefully, that would distract Westengaard long enough for Peter to get Flora out.

Westengaard let out a laugh. He turned around, playing to the enraptured crowd. "Falsely imprisoned by naïve country folk. This noble young woman saw through the lies and risked everything to free me. She was exiled, cast out for my sake. We travelled together, hoping for our future. I left her in safety while I gathered supplies. Then, I met Miss Winkleston, and she captured me with her lies and spells."

Peter snorted. "You abandoned Flora, and tricked Miss Winkleston. I know both these ladies, and they're nice people. Why are you doing this to such nice people? You're just a…"

Flora gripped Peter's arm and whispered, "The Culparr mines… they have made his powers weak, but he is still a warlock."

"You do not believe the truth about Miss Winkleston?" Westengaard said to the rapt audience. Adeline sat crumpled on the ground, tears making a smear of her makeup. "All of you will see the lies she and her foster father have been hiding all these years, appearing friendly and kind while participating in the darkest evils."

He swept his arm toward a wall of curtains along the side of the tent. They cascaded to the ground, and he grinned in triumph. Peter blinked, wondering why each pedestal was empty. On the last pedestal lay Rompell's scarf. Westengaard's jaw tightened, fury pulsing in his eyes.

Keeping hold of Flora's hand, Peter said, "Well, Flora and I really should be going… Good day."

He pulled Flora with him as he moved to pass Westengaard.

Remaining in their path, Westengaard said, "Nerrelanthia, tell them the truth. Confirm what I say."

"I think that's enough, sir," a white-haired gentleman said, stepping from the crowd. "I've known Adeline Winkleston since she was a girl at the Bradford School. She even taught my little Nancy. She's a fine lady, not a witch. What sort of gentleman are you, making such a scene?"

Peter made it past Westengaard as others joined Adeline's defense, building into an uproar. Flora clung tightly to Peter, pressing her head against his shoulder. Westengaard pushed past the crowd forming around him.

"Peter! No!" Flora shoved Peter into an archway of flowers.

Thunder snapped as lightning flashed from Westengaard's hand. Reminding himself how to breathe, Peter grabbed one of the smoke snaps from his pocket. Guests screamed and tumbled as they fainted throughout the hall. Peter motioned for Flora to drop to the ground. As they both lay flat, he threw the snap toward Westengaard.

Purple smoke snarled out, obscuring the warlock. Chairs toppled and crashed as the guests rushed toward the doors. Peter grabbed Flora's hand as they crawled into an abandoned row of chairs. She kissed him on the cheek, and then released his hand.

"I am sorry," she said. "Thank you, Peter, for everything."

She moved to stand, when he gripped her arm and said, "Where are you going? Havish and I've got a plan. We'll escape, leave the city if we have to."

"Peter, you can't fight a warlock."

"We don't need to. We just need to get out. Havish has a truck waiting. Come on."

Peter threw another smoke snap, and green smoke snarled through the air, mixing with the purple. Flora gripped his hand as they crouched behind chairs and scurried toward the nearest exit.

The smoke cleared, and Westengaard's eyes scanned the now broken tent. With a yell, he raised his hands and formed a ball of green light. He moved to launch it, when Peter threw another smoke snap. Yellow smoke formed around them, with sparks flying happily through the air. He and Flora leaped away. Westengaard's sphere of energy smashed into the chairs behind them, sending out a shockwave. Peter lost hold of Flora's hand as he fell. He turned to find her, but the smoke was too thick.

His heart jerked, and then he heard the whine of more magic forming. He pulled the hammer from beneath his pant leg and crawled till he was behind a massive floral arrangement, only a few arm lengths from Westengaard. The smoke cleared to a haze. Flora stood nearby in the aisle, quivering like a flower in a storm.

"Stop this, and I'll go with you," she said.

"Your purpose has failed." Westengaard strode toward her. "And you know too much. Goodbye, Nerrelanthia."

Flame wrapped around Westengaard's arm, just as it had when he had faced the rangers. Peter pulled himself into a crouch and tightened his hold on the hammer. Fire pooled out from Westengaard's arm, surrounding Flora. Peter tossed out a smoke snap, and blue smoke spread out.

"What do you think this child's magic will do?" Westengaard said with a laugh.

The fire singed Peter's clothes as he jumped through, hidden by the blue smoke. As he crept toward Westengaard's back, flames lapped at Flora's skirt. Flora held her head high as she sang a soft melody, a blue light forming around her, holding back the flame. Westengaard pushed forward his fist, and a pillar of flame surrounded Flora.

Finally close enough, Peter swung his hammer with full strength. The broad side slammed against the warlock's skull. Westengaard stumbled forward, and the pillar of flame lowered. He began to turn, when Flora grabbed a small pot of flowers from the floral arrangement. She threw it, the clay crashing against Westengaard. He shouted and the fire rose in fury, lighting the tent ceiling.

Peter swung the hammer again, landing it squarely against Westengaard's temple. The tall warlock shuffled like a drunken man, his feet moving in a loose circle. Peter hit him a third time, and Westengaard crashed to the ground.

The magical flame disappeared, but did not stop the natural fire now spreading across the tent. Chairs were lighting up as Flora grabbed Peter's arm.

"Adeline!" she said.

Coughing in the growing smoke, Peter kept hold of Flora's hand as he ran toward the stairs where Adeline lay, petrified by fear and shock. He was nearly there, when Rompell stepped in his way.

"Go," the Sandarian said as he pulled his foster daughter and her massive dress into his arms. "Thank you."

Trusting Adeline to Rompell, Peter and Flora sprinted through the nearest exit into the bright sunlight. Cries and shouts rose among the crowd as people pointed. The clang of a fire wagon rang from the city.

Peter turned his back on all this as he led Flora up the hill and to the street. Other guests pelted them with questions, but Peter and Flora pressed on, their hands wrapped tightly together.

At last, they reached where Havish leaned against his truck, a curious grin on his weathered face.

"Well," he said. "That was a bit of excitement."

Peter helped Flora into the back of the truck. He glanced down the hill just as the firefighters carried a singed Westengaard out on a gurney. Rompell stood close by, Adeline still in his arms as he spoke with a police officer. The Sandarian would take care of this mess. Peter needed to focus on Flora, just as Rompell had said.

Once Peter settled into the truck, Havish started the engine. The truck hummed and they rode away from the crowd and fire. A tingle ran through Peter's shoulder as Flora leaned into him, curling her legs beneath her. Her face was close to his, the light highlighting the curves of her face, neck, and long eyelashes. Even though his best pants were torn, top hat lost, and jacket soiled, Peter let himself smile.

When Peter Talbot bent his head to kiss Flora, he was not thinking of magic and fairytales. He was thinking of her perfect feet, of her delicate toes, of her round heel, of the curve of her fine arches, and how fine a shoe he would make for their wedding.

THE END

Acknowledgements

First, thank you to my writer's group in California led by the one and only Paul Bishop. Thank you for helping me learn where my writing strengths are, helping me have the courage to publish, and being fantastic people.

Second, thank you to of my beta readers and critique partners. In addition, I want to thank my editor, Summer Giles, and my editing consultant, Tara Forbush. Your insight has shown me blind spots and helped polish this book.

Third, thank you to my friends from summer camp, friends from home, and my 'other siblings' who have heard me talk for years about my stories. Thank you for listening and being patient while I have found my voice as a writer.

Fourth, thank you to the staff, faculty, and fellow students in my Masters in Public Administration program at BYU. Your trust and encouragement these past few months has been a huge support. I appreciate the many of you who say, "I'll buy your book," even without knowing what my book is about.

Fifth, thank you to my family for encouraging my creativity, providing honest – sometimes a bit too honest – feedback, and trusting in my talents and abilities. Julia, thanks for your book-business savvy, Katherine, your support and sharing your talents for the cover, Michael, thanks for being my nerd bro, Natalie, thanks for enduring all of my storytelling over the years, Alexis, for being excited about my stories, and Kayla, for being magical. Most of all, Mom and Dad, thanks for being supportive and being the backbone to help all of my siblings, other-siblings, and myself grow and be confident in ourselves.

About the Author

L. Palmer has spent many years traveling fictional worlds and building tales of grand, epic adventures. When she was in the midst of a grand battle between two ogres and a stegosaurus, she stumbled upon the world of Pippington. Dreams of wizard duels and clashing armies gave way to motorcars bumping down old city lanes and fairy godmothers disguised as high-society gossips. Here, she found a new literary home.

In between exploring the hidden lives and magic of Pippington, she lives among the mountains of Utah and attends graduate school at Brigham Young University. She developed her imagination and adventure skills through growing up in Girl Scouts, working for ten years at resident summer camps, teaching high school English, attending and working at the University of California Santa Barbara, and reading great books of fantasy and magic. The True Bride and the Shoemaker is just the beginning of many tales to come.

To learn more, visit **http://lpalmerchronicles.com**

Made in the USA
San Bernardino, CA
30 May 2015